A.C.H.E.

M. NEVER

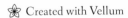

CONTENTS

ACHE. CHOICE. HIS. EVERLY.

USA TODAY BESTSELLING AUTHOR
M. NEVER

PROLOGUE

J

uliet
Age 16

"And what princess are you pretending to be tonight?" Tage slithers into my bedroom window like the cat burglar he is. It's dark. He's late. I'm impatient.

"When I'm with you, I'm not a princess, I'm a Capulet."

"So, I'm calling you Juliet?" He creeps across the room.

"That will do." I giggle softly as he skims across the top of my bedcovers and delivers a possessive, heart-stopping kiss. I thread my hands in his short, dirty-blond hair and hold on for dear life. I live for these clandestine moments. These secret rendezvous that are as dangerous as life and as imminent as death. Tage and I live in a perilous universe where violence rules and power reigns. We aren't supposed to know each other. Our paths were never intended to cross. He isn't supposed look at me or talk to me, let alone touch me.

I'm the Lladró in the glass curio cabinet left to look out over the world, alone. Separated, a precious porcelain figurine to be admired by one man, and one man alone.

"Did you miss me?" Tage asks as he sheds his leather jacket and then his shoes.

"Are you seriously asking that question?" I pull off my shirt and reveal my little pink, lace bra.

"I like to hear the answer." He covers me with his big, broad body.

"You know I did. I live for you," I squeak like a church mouse.

"I live for you," he professes, pressing his mouth to mine, swiping his tongue between my lips. An electrical charge passes through my entire body. It's a feeling only Tage can bring forth.

The first time he kissed me, I understood what it meant to be alive. For so long, I have been a doll. Propped in my pretty pink cage and hidden away from the world.

If anyone found out he was here, knew what we were involved in, or taking part in, he'd be executed like a prisoner of war. On the spot. No trial or jury, just guilty.

Tage knows the risks. He knew them the moment he laid eyes on me. He knew them as he silently stalked me for months. He knew them the night he crawled into my window and stole my first kiss. He knew them the night he took my virginity and uttered the words "I love you" — and he knows them now. We both do. Our relationship is treacherous, but it's undeniable. Incontestable, irrefutable. It's the air, and we suffocate when we're not together.

"How's my caged little bird?" Tage hooks his thumbs into the side strings of my panties. They're dainty and made entirely of lace. Much too mature for someone my age.

"She wants to be set free." I wiggle beneath his imprisoning body, helping him to rid the restrictive material as much as I can.

"Soon enough." He smothers me with a kiss while forcing my legs apart.

I fly higher and faster than a fighter jet as his essence seeps into my soul. As he brings me back to life. As my heart begins to beat and the apex of my thighs begins to pound.

I inhale fresh air for the first time today.

"I missed you," I sigh emphatically.

"I missed you, too. Every goddamn second." Tage's breathing quickens as the bulge beneath his zipper hardens rapidly. I love the pressure. The feel of the hard rod smashing against my pelvis.

I snake my hand between our bodies and pull at the button of his jeans, tugging until it comes loose and the whisper of metal teeth hisses.

"Ah," Tage groans gutturally as I stroke his erection. He taught me what he likes. Showed me how to touch him and what he's capable of when touching me. "Have you been taking your pills like a good girl?"

"Yes. Everyday, just like you told me." I hide my birth control in the lining of my mattress, right where he showed me.

"Good. Good girl. My girl." Tage kisses me between rasps, firmly, possessively, as he pushes his jeans down past his thighs.

"Are you wet for me?" He nudges the head of his erection against my entrance.

"Yes," I moan. "I've been thinking about you."

"And touching yourself?" He slides in just slightly.

"Yes," I huff. "Like you wanted."

"So, you're all ready for me?" He sinks all the way in and the wind is knocked out of me.

"Yes," I heave.

"Mmmm, baby, my baby." He circles his hips and the wall of my womb throbs.

"Tage," I whimper as I claw at his back. He's so much bigger than me, stronger, more powerful. When it comes to Tage, I'm his willing prisoner. And I want to be for the rest of my life.

I gasp as we fuck — wild and passionate, like it means life or death.

If we're not caught, it's life. If we are, it's death.

That tightness between my legs I associate only with Tage starts to pulsate. It spreads through my limbs like a pounding drum.

"Oh, God, oh, fuck." My words are swallowed by his hungry mouth eating away at mine.

"Shhh." He silences me with a French kiss so deep and demanding I drown in its dominance. I can't help it. I can't help the way he makes me feel or the response he elicits. I want to scream it to the world. I want to come loudly and freely like there's no consequence. But there is. A severe one. I calm myself, feeding off the slowing rhythm of Tage's hips. I am utterly enamored by this man.

He breaks the suffocating kiss and looks down at me with raw, hazel eyes. The brown ringing around his pupils is so dark and so deep. So captivating. I could stare into them forever.

"I was never supposed to fall in love with you, Juliet. But I did, and you've become mine." I flood with emotion. With hope. "I'm going to free you."

"When?" I plead desperately.

"Soon." He shivers, his climax threatening.

"What will happen to us?" My stomach muscles clench.

"We'll be together. And I promise, on my life, nothing will ever come between us." Tage pushes my body, my mind, and all my emotions.

"I want that." I cry as I come, spiraling down an orgasmic black hole.

"Oh, fuck, baby." He groans, tormented by the feel of my spasming pussy. "You'll get it. I promise, I'll take care of you. You'll never belong to anyone but me ever again. I'm the first man and the last man who'll ever touch you." Tage tenses, his last word lingering in the air as he finds his own earth-shattering release right behind mine.

Time stills as the man who means everything to me holds me tight, protects me, loves me. He's the first person in my entire life to show me real affection.

Relaxing after a few intense moments, Tage settles next to me on the mattress. I snuggle up to him, burying my face in his chest and inhale his signature scent. It's an intoxicating mix of tobacco and mint.

The room is silent and dark, and even though threat looms over us with every passing second, our stolen moments are worth more than diamonds or platinum or gold. Worth more than life, because I am certain, if he asked me to, I would die for this man.

Tage gave me something priceless.

Himself.

And I handed him back the only thing I owned that was of any value.

My heart.

"I love you," I murmur.

His arms tighten around me. "I love you more. I'll love you always." He presses a firm kiss to my head.

"Don't go." I hold on to him for dear life. "Every time you leave, another piece of me crumbles away." I have a ridiculous, childish fantasy that he becomes the monster who lives under my bed. And although he looks and sounds scary, he isn't there to hurt me, he's there to protect me.

"Do you trust me, Juliet?" Tage tilts my face up. It's hard to see his features in the dark, but I can feel his heavy eyes on me as if they were free weights. Of all the times we have been together — the months of sneaking around, the secret rendezvous, and stolen moments — he has never once asked me that question. Ever.

Do I trust him . . .?

"With my life."

"Good. Because your life is my main concern. It's my priority. My duty. And I need you to trust that I know what I'm doing. That I have a plan."

"Want to give me a few details of that plan?" I fish.

"I can't give you many. I can just tell you soon. Very, very soon." He swipes the pad of his thumb across my heated cheek.

Soon. That sounds so . . . hopeful. Tage is one of my stepfather's foot soldiers. He's a thief, and a liar, even a killer when he needs to be. I've been surrounded by men like that since I was seven. Since my sleazy, drug-addicted mother entered into a relationship with Malcolm "Gunner" Tremmall, a Chicago Southside drug runner who was quickly making a name for himself.

Eight years later, he's built one of the most lucrative drug-trafficking rings north of the Mason-Dixon line.

My life wasn't always this secluded, though. When we first moved into the compound, I had my freedom. I could roam when and where I wanted. Neither my mother nor my stepfather bothered with me much. They were both concerned with more important things — my mother getting high, and Gunner carving out his empire through intimidation and fear. He's no one to fuck with. It's clear by just the way he presents himself. He's an imposing figure. Tall, stoic, and ruthless as hell, with black eyes that are a perfect match to his black soul.

But one day, everything changed. Everything I had grown accustomed to was taken away from me. The little freedom I had, gone.

It happened right after my thirteenth birthday. It was like any other morning. I woke up, brushed my teeth in my *en suite* bathroom, and then tried to go downstairs for breakfast. *Tried* being the operative word. Two of Malcolm's huge goons were guarding the door, and when I attempted to walk past them, they stopped me. *Blocked me*. I couldn't understand what was going on. I never really received an explanation either. From that day forward, I became a prisoner. Sentenced to spend my life alone, in solitude, in an elegant prison decorated in pink and white. I was Rapunzel, minus the long blonde hair, staring out at the world from the window of my tower. And for three years, that's how I lived, secluded, until the night Tage Andrews appeared and changed everything. Changed me.

I had seen him many times walking across the courtyard — a paved square in the middle of the property surrounded by beautiful climbing vines in the summer and snow-covered grounds in the winter — and every now and again the path of our eyes would meet. Only for a fleeting second, but the connection was like fire. For me,

anyway. I don't know how many times it happened, countless probably, but I felt his stare touch the same place inside me every single
time. Deep in my core, it kindled my insides in ways I didn't understand but became addicted to. I would search him out, just to feel that
little flash of excitement. I began to live for it, and soon, live for him. I
didn't even know his name. He was a stranger, a mystery that occupied my mind. A person I could never touch, or meet, or talk to. But
that all changed the night he climbed into my window. The night he
altered everything, my entire existence.

One kiss possessed me. One kiss turned a fixation into an
infatuation.

I watch quietly as Tage drags up his jeans and zippers his fly. My
heart deflates. I don't want him to go. It's getting harder and harder to
watch him leave. To be alone.

"Please don't go yet." I reach for him desperately. Tage grabs my
hand and plops back down on the bed.

"Soon, I'll never have to leave." He traps my face and embraces
me wildly, one wet, starving, paralyzing kiss right after another. I'm
light-headed by the time he's done, and dizzy with so many emotions.
"Be patient, Juliet, promise me."

"I promise," I sigh. "I'd wait forever for you."

"That's what I want to hear." Tage stands, and I sag. *Please don't
go.* "I'll be back before you know it."

"You promise?" I stare up at him. His strong frame is highlighted
by the moonlight pouring in through the windows.

"Yes. You promise, I promise." He drops a kiss on my freckled
nose.

I nod. I trust him. With everything I am. With everything I have.

Tage slithers out of the room the same way he came in, like a cat.
Like a thief, making off with my heart.

Once he's out of sight, I spring out of bed and grab a pink sheet of
paper and a pen off my desk. I scribble a few words down, then fold
the paper into an airplane. I rush to the window and call out in a
hushed tone, "Tage!" I send the pink paper airplane soaring in his

direction, and he catches it right before it crashes into the ground. Then he's gone. Swallowed by the darkness.

I climb into bed, playing the events of the night over and over like I always do. It helps me hold on, helps me stay sane.

"Soon, Juliet." I hear Tage's words echo around me. Soon.

THE SOUND of a gunshot startles me awake. Another prompts me to scurry out of bed and crawl to the window. I peek out of the glass from the floor to find Gunner pointing a gun at Tage. Tage is crawling on all fours across the courtyard, clearly injured. I want to scream, but fear is choking my vocal chords. I watch helplessly as Gunner stalks Tage under the faint moonlight. I can't hear what he's saying, but I can see the gun glint as he moves. My eyes sting from prickly tears, and my heart is beating so fast my chest feels like it's cracking.

Please no, please no, please no is all I can think. It's a drumline beating through my head.

The world becomes blurry as the onslaught of tears cloud my vision.

Please God, take anything or anyone except Tage.

Another gunshot rings out and my nails break against the windowsill. My world shatters. I hear screaming, but it's so far and removed it takes me a second to realize it's me. It's my voice, my pain, my anguish, projecting from my own throat.

Then there's chaos. Bright lights, loud swooshing sounds, and a man's voice raining down through a loudspeaker.

I wipe my eyes, trying to find my bearings. So much so fast. A helicopter hovers over the courtyard with the letters "FBI" accented in gold. People with guns flood the courtyard, and Gunner's crew seem to scatter like rats. I'm terrified, frozen in place, watching the one and only person I care about die on the cold ground.

As I'm suspended in time, my door is kicked open, and more men in black invade my bedroom. There must be ten of them. They're bigger than life and crowd the spacious room. One scoops me up, but I grab onto the windowsill. I can't go. I can't leave Tage, not like that. Alone. Dying.

"Save him!" I scream as they tear me away. "You have to save him!" I flail in the stranger's arms in a fit of panic, reaching for the window.

For Tage.

For my heart.

For my life.

For my everything.

1

E verly
  Eight years later
  Present day

"I swear to fucking God, if I didn't like Mr. Turner so much, I'd quit." Lara spins in her chair and glares at me.

"Another 'special request'?" I giggle.

"They are superlative submissions according to him. Leave it to a lawyer to eloquently rename bitch work." She slams a stack of papers on our shared desk.

"But no one does bitch work like you." I bat my eyelashes at her mockingly.

"Apparently not, because not one other secretary in this firm has to confirm with one hundred names on the guest list for the company party tonight. That's what he has a party planner for," she hisses.

"There's not one other secretary sleeping with a junior partner either," I sing softly.

Lara straightens in her chair. "Do you think he knows? Are Luke and I that obvious?" she whispers conspiratorially.

"No, I just think Mr. Turner is fond of you. You're not a dumb blonde."

"Neither are you," she argues.

"I haven't been here as long, and he trusts you."

Lara sighs. "It has been an age, and I'm only twenty-seven." She curls her pretty pink lips.

I met Lara six months ago when I was hired at Turner Simon and Hooch. It's one of the premier law firms in New York City. High-class, high-end, high-profile all the way. Intimidating? Hell yeah. Awesome? Also, hell yeah. The perks and bonuses are amazing, and I'm only a secretary. Partners and junior partners? Sky's the limit. If there's an event, sport, or concert, the lawyers here have every privilege. Boxing match in Las Vegas? Take the private jet. Offshore fishing expedition? Use the private yacht. Annual Christmas party? We'll see you at a penthouse three floors higher than the top of the Rock. The shit is bananas, and the best job I have ever had. Which is why I choose to lay low, and that's more than I can say for my counterpart. She loves to walk on the wild side. In this instance, the wild side I'm referring to would be Luke Dunham — a tall, dark, and handsome up-and-coming junior partner currently making a name for himself. All eyes are on him and a few other all-stars in the firm. They started hooking up right around the time I got the job. Lara was friendly enough, and we hit it off right away. A few weeks later, I came to find out she was having an affair with Luke. Warning bells went off since I was lectured long and hard by my personnel rep on the repercussions of fraternizing in the workplace. The firm has a zero-tolerance policy. Both employees are automatically terminated if discovered. They aren't overly strict about many things, but they're sticklers about this.

"You're right. You are only twenty-seven. You have a long career ahead of you."

"Are you hinting I should be more careful?" She sways back and forth in her chair.

I shrug as I pull a piece of peach licorice from the package. "I'm not hinting anything. You're interpreting." I nibble innocently on the sweet tip.

"I hate when you pull that psychoanalytical shit on me, Ever."

"I'm not pulling anything." I stifle a laugh. I'm full of shit, and we both know it. "Licorice?" I offer.

"Ugh, no." Lara rolls her eyes and organizes the stack of papers in front of her. "I don't know how you eat those crappy things."

"They're delish."

"They're gonna rot your teeth."

"I go to the dentist." I chew.

"Nice to know you leave the house for more than just work," she digs.

I stick my tongue out at her. "Just because I'm not having an affair with a junior partner doesn't mean I don't have a life."

"Do you have a life?" Lara counters.

I grimace. Why does she have to hassle me?

"Well?" she pushes. I want to kick her.

"No," I gripe. But that's my choice.

I retreat into myself, going back to concentrating heavily on my computer screen. For a half second, while Lara and I were joking, I felt normal. Felt light, but it always creeps back — the past, my hindrances, my impairments. Loneliness is like a crutch. A handicap I'm cursed to live with.

"It doesn't have to be that way, Ever. You don't have to have an illicit affair to have a life. You just need to leave your apartment." Her tone is soft. Consoling almost.

"I leave my apartment, Lara." I agitatedly grab for another piece of licorice.

"For more than work." Her chair squeaks as she turns her body in my direction. She's wearing a light-pink pantsuit that compliments her complexion perfectly. Lara is classically beautiful, with long, blonde hair, big, blue eyes, and sharp facial features. It's like working alongside career woman Barbie sometimes. I, on the other hand, have mossy-green eyes, freckles splattered across my nose, and auburn hair I dye dark brown. We're starkly different in looks but have the exact same taste in almost everything else. It's part of the reason we get along so well. Most of the time.

"Are you going to the company party tonight?" She's trying to make a point by asking that loaded question.

"No." I don't look at her.

"Why not?"

"Because." It's the lamest excuse on the planet, and she knows it.

"Because," she spits. "Because, because, because. Can you at least come up with something better than that?"

"Nope." I'm belligerent.

Lara sighs loudly, purposely voicing her annoyance. I don't know what she wants from me. I'm fucking damaged, plain and simple. A defective product of my destructive past.

"You're going," she informs me.

"Says who?" I swing my face in her direction.

"Says me. I say. You are going. I'm not going to let you waste away in your apartment tonight, having a one-sided conversation with your cat."

"I love Denali," I moan.

"I'm sure you do, but you also need human interaction. You need to indulge in gourmet food, sip expensive champagne, and appreciate a spectacular view of Manhattan," Lara speaks enthusiastically. She is clearly looking forward to tonight.

"I have nothing to wear." I toss out another lame-ass excuse.

"Bullshit," she snorts. "I know what's in your closet. I know how much money you spend on clothes that never see the light of day. It's like a damn vintage museum in your closet."

Fuck, this bitch knows me too damn well. I do have a weakness for name brands.

"Lara—"

"Don't, Everly." She holds up her hand, silencing me. "I'm not taking no for an answer. You're going, end of story. I will rip you out of your apartment if I have to."

"That sounds unpleasant."

"It will be, if it comes to that." For Christ's sake. I inwardly bristle. "I refuse to let you become a reclusive old cat lady."

"Why do you care so much?"

"Because I'm your friend. And friends meddle." She smiles obnoxiously.

"You are definitely meddling," I strongly agree, reaching for another piece of licorice. I chomp irritably, hating the fact that I'm being bullied — even if Lara does have good intentions.

"Fuck." She nearly jumps out of her chair. "Four-thirty already."

"Um, yeah. We usually work till five." I regard her like she's nuts.

"I know, but I'm leaving early today. I have a hair and makeup appointment. I want to look amazing tonight." Lara races around gathering her purse and cell phone while she shuts down her computer. "I want Luke salivating every time he looks at me."

"That's just mean."

"I know." She pauses and smirks deviously.

"Playing with fire," I remind her.

"If all goes well, I won't need to worry about losing my job 'cause I'll be able to quit."

"What, why?" I snatch her arm.

"'Cause Luke has been dropping hints. We're getting really serious, Ever. He might just be the one."

"Seriously?" My eyebrows shoot up. "Why didn't you tell me this sooner?" I feel a little hurt.

"Well, we can't exactly have girl talk in the middle of the office about my forbidden relationship. And I have to literally drag you out for drinks after work."

Fair enough. But still, I want to know. I want Lara to be able to confide in me. I want a friend. I don't know what epiphany suddenly strikes me, but I make a rash decision. "Okay," I give in. "I'll go to the party tonight."

Lara laughs, cackles almost. "Oh, honey, I know. You never had a choice. I already RSVP'd for you. I wasn't kidding when I said I would rip you out of your apartment. Now, make sure you dress up all pretty, and I'll see you tonight. 'Kay?" She bounces in her spiked heels.

"'Kay," I rumble.

"You spend way too much time with your cat, you're starting to sound like him." Lara starts for the elevator before stopping dead in her tracks. "Can you do one thing for me?" She picks up a thick blue folder next to her computer. "Can you drop this in Alec's office before you go? I highlighted everything he asked me to. Took me almost all day."

"Alec?" I curl my lip. "Alec Stewart?"

"Nope," she chirps. "Alec Prescott."

I groan. Anyone but him. "I thought you were my friend."

"I am." Her voice elevates. "I promise I'll make it up to you. I'll buy you drinks all night." She hightails it out of the office.

"It's open bar!" I yell.

But it's too late, she's gone.

Fucker.

I put off going to Alec's office as long as I can. I really can't stand the man. He's frigid as fuck and condescending as hell. I try to avoid the pompous asshole as much as possible. Cold and calculating is probably what makes him so good at his job, but it does nothing for his social standing.

Sometimes, I wonder if he possesses any humanity at all.

I walk down the carpeted hallways, clutching the blue folder to my chest. I'm going to make this quick. A drive by drop off with minimal interaction.

The door to his office is shut and all the blinds are pulled closed — a subliminal *fuck off*.

I inhale a deep breath and knock on the door. Here we go.

"Come in." His low timber vibrates through the wood. I enter, still holding my breath, and walk swiftly to his desk. He doesn't even look up as I stand there. It's like I'm invisible, a tribulation, nothing of importance at all.

A silent moment passes. I don't know what I'm waiting for. Neither does he, because Alec finally looks up, his icy blue eyes cutting right through me. I push my reading glasses up my nose and fidget a bit. I wish he wasn't so fucking attractive. He's got all the damn goods. Smart, handsome, rich, too bad he loses major points for being a grade-A asshole.

"Is that for me?" His question is short, curt.

"Um, yes." I hand him the folder. "Lara asked me to drop it off."

"And where is she?" He flips open the folder and inspects the contents. He's so critical for a second that I fear for Lara's job.

"She left early. She needed a little extra time to get ready for the party tonight," I divulge, questioning if it was smart to share.

Alec grunts. I'm not sure why. Maybe because he thinks she's slacking. Half the office left early, so I don't see the big deal. We're basically the only two left. What does that say about us?

No lives?

Workaholics?

Antisocial?

All of the above?

Probably.

Definitely for me.

Alec just shakes his head as he looks over Lara's highlights.

That is my cue to go.

I turn on my heel to leave. My blood has turned into an icy stream from just being in his presence.

"Aren't you going to the party?" Alec asks, detached. I glance over my shoulder.

"Yes," I squeak, then clear my throat.

"Then why are you still here?"

"Why are you?" I don't know what compels me to fire back. Maybe it's because I hate the way he talks to me. The way he talks to everyone. I'm rebelling, stupidly.

Alec pauses, lifting his bold, blue eyes slowly as I turn to face him.

My pulse pounds in my ears as he looks me over. He is so fucking intimidating, but I'm not going to cower. Not on the outside anyway.

"I brought my change of clothes to the office. Allows me to work longer," he shares evenly. He's so eerily calm and collected I want to check to see if he even has a pulse.

"I guess most people aren't as smart or as dedicated as you."

"They're definitely not." I may be imagining it, but I think he's smirking. The lift of his lips is so faint I have to stare to make sure the curve is actually there. "Don't you need some extra time to get ready?" Alec inquires.

"No. I can change quickly. It doesn't take much for me to get ready."

"Clearly." He deliberately cocks an eyebrow at me. I glance down at myself. I'm dressed in neat work attire. A pair of slim black pants, black high heels, and a white, striped, button-up shirt. It's freakin' Calvin Klein. Why is he judging?

"Is there anything else?" I bite.

"Nope." He looks back down at his paperwork, all but dismissing me.

Prick.

I march out of his office, closing the door a little harder than I mean to. But what the fuck, who cares? Not me.

I shutdown my computer, grab my purse, and get the hell out of the office.

I have a party to get ready for.

2

E verly

IN MY BEDROOM, I stare at myself in the mirror. All I keep hearing is Alec's condescending reply.

Clearly.

Clearly.

Clearly.

I flick the end of one of my braids and fluff my dark bangs. I don't have a stitch of makeup on, and my glasses are sitting on the brim of my freckled nose. My outfit is nice, but there isn't much more to me. I see what he sees.

Nothing special.

My heart is heavy, but my determination is burning bright. I want more, I just have to be brave enough to reach for it. The last few years have been challenging. I dug myself out of a dark place, and I am just now starting to see the light.

"You can do this," I give myself a pep talk. "You can be more. You deserve more." Those words burn my tongue. They're hinged by heartache. A heartache I've been carrying around for eight, long years.

I shake off the sorrow. Tonight is about fun. And what's more fun than playing dressing up? For me, not much.

I wash quickly, then pick out my dress. My closet is packed with designer clothes, most with the tags still on them. I love to shop but am limited on places to go. That doesn't stop me from blowing half of my paycheck on brand names. I know exactly what I want to wear. The red, sexy cocktail dress is shoulder-baring with a slit up the side. It leans much more to the side of sophisticated than skank. I can't show up to an elite office party looking like a prostitute. The clincher for me was the tied, off-the-shoulder sleeves. They're so feminine and chic, the bows dangling on my arms add the perfect, classy embellishment.

Paired with a nude, strappy heel, the outfit is perfect for the night.

I spend a little extra time on my makeup. Just because I don't wear it often doesn't mean I don't have any. I smoke my eyes out with black shadow and swipe my lashes with several coats of black mascara. Finally, I loosen my hair from the two braids, and it falls in loose, tousled waves around my shoulders.

I barely recognize myself by the time I'm all said and done.

The girl staring back at me in the mirror now is a polar opposite to the one from earlier today. To the one every day.

I grab my purse and order up an Uber on my way down to the lobby. My apartment complex isn't anything extravagant, but it has a doorman, and it's safe. Living in the city is expensive as hell, so scoring something halfway affordable in a decent neighborhood is like winning the lottery.

The white Accord picks me up on the sidewalk and whisks me away to Uptown. The firm's party is in their company suite sixty floors above the ground. The view of Manhattan is absolutely spectacular and so is the space itself. All floor-to-ceiling windows, a huge balcony, and an ultra-clean, neoclassical design. White marble, Roman columns, and extravagant décor. I've only been here once before, for a Valentine's Day function the firm held when I first started. I learned quickly these events are legendary.

I steel my nerves as the elevator doors open to a bustling room filled with high-profile clientele and all my peers.

As soon as I step into the room I'm offered champagne by a waiter wearing a tuxedo and white gloves balancing a silver tray full of bubbling flutes.

I accept graciously. I'm going to need all the alcohol I can get my hands on tonight.

The whole atmosphere is beyond upscale. It's distinguished and impressive, and sometimes I can't believe I'm actually part of this world — considering my shady upbringing. But that's all in the past. The only place I'm looking now is the future. At least, I'm trying to.

I peruse through the room admiring the beautiful detail of the molding on the walls as I look for Lara. I know she's here somewhere.

"Miss Paige?" Caught admiring the huge chandelier above my head, I hear my name. I look down to find Mr. Turner regarding me warmly. He's an older man with wild grey hair, smile lines, and crow's feet. He's supposedly a pit pull in the courtroom, but I've only ever known him to be a big puppy dog.

"Mr. Turner." I smile.

"I'm so glad you came." He returns my expression tenfold.

"I hate to miss a party." *Lie.*

"Well, I'm so glad we have a chance to chat. I wanted to ask if you've seen the applications for the paralegal opportunity."

"Umm, the ones about applying for school?" I wrack my brain. I know something came through my email.

"Yes, that exact one. Every so often the firm offers a higher learning opportunity to its employees. I thought you might be an excellent candidate. You're very smart, always well organized, and I believe you would represent the firm well." He beams, and I'm floored.

"Really?" I've never considered being anything more than just a secretary, but a compliment — and recommendation — from one of the founding partners has me reeling.

"Really." He emphasizes with a nod. Mr. Turner is so mild-mannered it's hard to picture him as cut-throat as his reputation proceeds.

"I'll consider it."

"Fine, fine." He nods some more, continuing to smile. "Just remember, opportunity presents itself, but it doesn't last forever." He clicks his champagne glass with mine.

"I will definitely keep that in mind," I promise.

"Good. You look lovely, by the way. Enjoy yourself, Miss Paige." He winks good-naturedly before rejoining his party.

Now, why can't Alec act more like Mr. Turner? Cordial in a social setting and an attack dog in the courtroom. I'm sure it would do wonders for his personal life.

"Ever!" Lara hisses my name. I turn to find her decked out in a black cocktail dress with a plunging neckline detailed with diamonds. Damn, she went all out.

"Trying to get someone's attention?" I drip my fingertip into the opening of her dress.

"Damn right." She slides her eyes over to Luke, who's standing next to the intricately molded mantel in the main living room. He can't pull his attention away from her, even though he is trying to desperately stay engaged in the conversation going on with some of the other junior partners, Alec included.

He's failing miserably, though. It's clear all he wants is Lara.

"You two are going to set the building on fire if you keep looking at each other like that." I step in front of her, blocking his view.

"We can't help it." She peeks her head around me. "It's like . . . gravity or something. I can't control it. I just want him all the damn time."

I'm familiar with that feeling, even if it's been an eternity since I actually experienced it. That connection, that pull. The whole world disappears, and the only thing left is you and him and the electricity the two of you create.

My chest aches from the memory. From the crater formed by the devastation of the past.

"Just be careful. Your attraction is way obvious," I warn her. "You can't get fired. You're my sanity at work."

Lara smiles at me, her big, blue eyes shining. "I'm not going to get fired, but I may have to quit."

"Not without a ring on your finger." I'm attempting to be the voice of reason. "Don't throw your whole career away for a crush."

"Everly." Lara bites her lip. "I don't think this is a crush. It's the real thing. He told me he loved me. That he wants to be with me. And I sure as hell want to be with him." She's like a love-struck puppy in a designer dress.

I sigh. "Just as long as you know what you're doing."

"I hope I do, 'cause I am ready to throw everything away for him."

"What about him? Would he throw everything away for you?"

Lara slides her eyes over to me. "I think he would. You don't know the afternoon we had. The sex," she whispers. "It was on another level. We connected in a brand-new way. It was amazing. Life-changing. And then he told me, no, he professed how much he loved me. I've never been happier. I've never wanted someone so much," she gushes.

Have you ever been so happy for someone it actually makes you hate them? I despise what I'm feeling right now. I'm thrilled Lara found love, but I'm also jealous as hell at the exact same time. I want what she has. I want it back. That feeling of freedom, of invincibility. There's nothing like it, the addiction, the high. But when you lose it, the detox is debilitating.

I've swam through Heaven, and I've crawled through Hell, and for the last eight years, I've lingered in Purgatory. Drifting, trying to find my way through this isolating world. But I don't want to be alone anymore. I want to put myself out there. It's time. I'm twenty-four years old, and I've finally decided to dig myself out of my own grave.

I want more.

I *deserve* more.

Sometimes you don't think you're worthy, and then one day you wake up and realize you are. And that tiny bit of empowerment can spark a change. My spark is small, but I'm working like hell to start a fire.

Am I scared? Yes. Terrified, actually. But fear has crippled me long enough. My desire has grown stronger than my dread.

And I want what Lara has. Starry eyes and butterflies and happiness. I want happiness. Real, tried-and-true happiness. Nothing sugar-coated. No complications or smoke and mirrors, just something genuine. Something simple. Someone to kiss at midnight on New Year's Eve, to open presents with on Christmas morning. Someone to turn to in good times and bad. Someone I don't have to miss.

Someone — something — tangible. Touchable.

Real.

I want real.

I down my champagne before grabbing another glass from one of the silver trays being serviced around the room. I stand next to Lara quietly as she eye-fucks Luke for a good portion of the night. By my third glass of champagne, I'm antsy. There is a cluster of people I don't know around me, and Lara is gravitating toward Luke as his coworker clan slowly dissipates. Soon, he's alone, and Lara is headed straight for him. Their attraction is so blatant you could see it from Mars. As much as I adore Lara, I want no part of their little romance. Their affair is detrimental to all involved. And I'd like to avoid losing my job on account of being guilty by association.

As Lara makes her way to one side of the white marble fireplace dominating the living room, I make a beeline in the opposite direction for the balcony. I'm dying for some fresh air and a few collective minutes alone.

3

lec

I INHALE A LONG, hard pull from my vape pen, holding the sweet tasting weed vapor in my lungs before releasing a large cloud of smoke. I watch the grey tendrils dance in front of my face before rising above my head and dissipating into the blackened night sky.

Fucking placidity. For a fraction of a second, my mind is calm. It's slow, and unruffled, and undisturbed. I inhale again, the lights of Upper Manhattan twinkling for miles right before my eyes.

All the high with none of the judgement or repercussion. Just a pleasantly innocent aroma of fresh-baked cookies wafting through the atmosphere.

I zone out, leaning on the balcony as my mind takes a hiatus. I don't have long, a few precious minutes to myself before it's back to the grind, rubbing elbows with senior partners and hobnobbing with high-profile clients. Pretentious is an understatement, but it's a crucial part of the job.

I exhale another large cloud of smoke, and as it clears around me, the figure of a woman materializes in my peripheral vision. The sharp curves of her silhouette catch my attention, and as I slowly turn my head, so much more seizes my mind. Her big, green eyes capture me. The look in them dreamy, as if she just woke up, yet so vigil they penetrate right through me. A strange silence surrounds her, like it's haunting her. Haunting us both. I forget to breathe, and when my lungs recognize the thinning oxygen, I inhale. I inhale *her*. I breathe her right in and feel her everywhere. Her essence assaults me like a hallucinogen, rushing through my bloodstream, affecting me like a drug. A drug so much stronger than anything I have ever experienced. And I've experienced the spectrum. I know what a high is, and this is something on a completely different level. No words are exchanged, no verbal interaction, just a moment shared between two people caught in a time lapse. She seems familiar, but I can't put my finger on how I know her. *If* I know her. I must. There's an intimate air about her. But a woman as stunning as her I would surely remember. The brief time in her presence has been burned into my soul. I absorb her, my psyche floating over every inch of her body, consuming her curves, memorizing the features of her face, the pattern of her freckles lightly splattered on her cheeks and over her nose, the movement in the waves of her long, brown hair, and the gold flecks glinting like shards of glass in her sharp, emerald eyes.

There's four feet of space between us, and I want there to be none. I want to be closer. The attraction building is a raging firestorm, and the only thing that will calm the flames is her hands on me. Her hands all over me, and mine all over her. Something throbs inside me as I take one slow step closer. I can't stop myself. It's compulsive, the need to be nearer to her.

The environment enhances around us as I take yet another step. The building lights are twinkling a little bit brighter, the night sky is circling like in a Van Gogh, and the smell of her skin is as potent as a prize-winning rose conservatory. It's a wild dreamscape encased in stale reality.

Her swift intake of oxygen is as clear and concise as an axe swinging through the air. And all I want is to steal her breath away to keep it for myself.

Her rosy lips part just as I come into reaching distance, and that's when I realize . . .

"Ever!" A shrill voice cuts through the haze. "I've been looking for you." Lara stops short when she finds Everly with me. Not that we're technically together. We're technically nothing, just two acquaintances standing way too close.

"Um . . ." Everly fucking Paige bats her long eyelashes at me before giving her friend her full attention. When did the bland secretary become the fiery siren? "I was just getting some air." Her soft voice sends multiple kinds of chills down my spine.

"Well, come on." Lara snatches her hand, yanking her close, and whispers something in her ear. Her smile is way too devilish.

Everly's eyes widen. She bites her lip as Lara drags her away. I want to reach out and grab her. Roar possessively at Lara to leave her with me. But I don't. I keep composed, clinging on to the last moments of my out-of-body experience.

Everly throws me a strange look over her shoulder just before she disappears inside. I understand the expression. I don't know what the fuck that was either, siren. But I liked it. And I want more. So much fucking more.

Of all the women in all the world — Everly fucking Paige, the girl who's plain Jane, Blah Betty, and totally off limits is my original fucking high.

And as I breathe in another lungful of vapor, I'm left with only one question that matters . . . how the fuck do I get her alone again?

4

E verly

I STICK my key in the lock right before dawn. Lara kept me out all freakin' night, clubbing with her and Luke and a few other errant employees who like to break the rules. Luckily, Alec was nowhere to be found. I shiver as I turn the key, reliving that oddball encounter on the balcony of the firm's loft. The way he was looking at me. With those wild, piercing blue eyes. It's like he'd never seen a woman before.

Weird does not begin to describe that man.

I drop my clutch on the table, kick the door closed, and in a zombie state head straight for my bedroom. Sleep. Now, I internally whine. The crack of sun breaking through the horizon burns my tired eyes, but it's the voice that flits through the room that really reduces me to ash.

"Late night?" His tone is soft but firm, and oh so judgmental.

"I'm a big girl. I can come home when I want." I can barely stand up straight, my knees fighting against the edge of the mattress to keep me vertical. I just want to face plant into my pillow and pass out. That doesn't look like it's in my foreseeable future.

"I know you are." My visitor shifts in the corner. Arms and legs crossed, lounging comfortably against the wall.

"How long have you been standing there?" I eye him.

"A while." He isn't amused.

I couldn't care less if he is or isn't. He could stand there for eternity for all I give a shit.

"Maybe drop a note next time you feel like blowing back into town. I'll make sure to take a vacation so you don't have to bother *visiting* me."

Not a muscle on his body twitches in response to my scathing reply.

I don't affect him at all. In hindsight, I realize I never did. "What do you want, Tage?" I get right to the point. Sleep is calling to me, and I'm in no mood to entertain him. I'm in no mood to entertain anyone.

"I need to check up on you. It's my job."

"Checking up on me hasn't been your job in a very long time." I'm twenty-four, for Christ's sake. I've been surviving on my own without him for long enough.

"Checking up on you will always be my job." Tage pushes off the wall and strides toward me. My bedroom is small, so it only takes him three large steps to settle beside me. Too close. I inhale a collective breath as indiscreetly as I can. I don't want him to know he still affects me. That some days I still ache for him so badly it brings tears to my eyes. He broke my fucking heart and left me holding all the shattered pieces. There are still scars on my palm and a hole in my chest from the wreckage.

"Maybe it's time you take up a new career." I cross my arms and stand strong. He will not topple me. He will not see.

"Never." Tage tickles the bow dangling against my arm. My skin erupts into goosebumps, and I bite down on my tongue to stop myself from screaming at him.

I hate you.

I love you.

I wish I had never met you.

"You look . . ." The sentence hangs in the atmosphere.

"Perfectly fine without you...?" I take the liberty of finishing for him.

"...*breathtaking.*" He invokes his own liberties and corrects me.

The single word stabs me square in the heart.

I don't respond. I can't bring myself to even utter a small thank you.

I stare straight ahead, counting the divots in my comforter. It's the only thing that can keep my mind occupied. The only thing that can block him out. *Why is he doing this? Why now? Why at all? Why couldn't he just walk away and stay away?* Every time I see him, the half-healed wound gets ripped wide open, and all the suppressed feelings — the devastation, the heartache, the pain — shoots right back up to the surface.

Please leave and never come back.

I silently wish it but don't have the balls to say it.

Just let me move on.

I steal one last look at Tage. His golden-blond hair is a long wavy mess on the top of his head, there are bags under his gorgeous, hazel eyes, and his T-shirt is dirty. It makes me wonder what he's been up to. I never know. I never know where he goes or what he does when he disappears for months at a time, and I never know when he's going to reappear again.

He's a mystery. He always has been, since the moment we met. But regardless of the time that's passed, he still bewitches me as much now as he did back then.

"Are we done here?" I clear my throat, feeling very exposed from the way he's ingesting me with his eyes.

Don't look at me like that. You lost that right. A long time ago.

"For now." His fingertip brushes against my sensitive skin for a fraction of a second, and the world heats up. It's suddenly the tropics in my tiny city apartment, warm and humid and on the brink of a hurricane.

5

T age

Everly fucking hates me.

Hate? No, that word isn't fractionally strong enough. Loathes, despises, detests would describe her feelings much more accurately. She has every right to feel the way she does. What I did to her was wrong. I made a promise, and although I kept it on a certain level, it came nowhere near to the expectation she had. Not even close.

And I pay a hefty price for that deception every damn day.

Every damn time I look into those broken green eyes. *I* did that. But it was for her own good. At least, that's what I told myself all those years ago. *She's better off without me.* It's what I've continually told myself until this very day, until this very minute, but even as I try to convince myself now, I'm second-guessing my decision. Maybe even regretting it.

Everly Paige has turned into the woman I saw inside her eight long years ago. When I seduced an innocent teenager, who beguiled me before I even realized it. She beguiles me just as much now as an adult. Maybe even more so.

I've fought my feelings for so long, and for what? What was I protecting her from back then? Me? The world? Her past? The truth? What am I protecting her from now?

I thought she could have a better life without me, but was that selfless decision made in vain? Was it really selfless at all? Was it more selfish? Was my career more important than the girl I loved? Is it still now? Have I bettered myself over the last eight years or just matured into the dickhead I was always destined to be? I wanted more for Everly.

More than me.

But now, I wonder if I'm enough. If she could truly love the man I am and not the figment from the past.

I've done a number of courageous things. Put myself in the line of fire, faced some of the most evil people on Earth, committed despicable acts all in the name of justice. But confronting the feelings I've been harboring inside me for eight years feels like laying on top of an atomic bomb.

What if I'm not enough?

What if I'm not worthy enough?

Everly deserves every star in the galaxy. Her past is riddled with pain. And for a short time, I eased that pain. But for the last eight years, I was just another cause.

I bang my head lightly on her closed front door. I want to rush back inside and declare my wants, my needs. I want to be the man I once was with her. A rebel. Uninhibited. Her everything.

I sigh heavily, my chest tightening from stress. One day. One day very soon, Everly Paige will once again be mine.

6

E verly

Do you ever feel like your life is just a set of revolving doors? In, around, and out, day after day. Time seems to bleed together, and you find yourself in the exact same place over and over wondering exactly how you got there? That has felt like my existence for as long as I can remember. If it's not one series of events, it's another. I order the same exact thing from Perks — the coffee shop right next door to my office building — as I do every morning. A caramel macchiato with extra foam. My hair is in braids, my glasses are resting on the brim of my nose, and my outfit is business casual conservative, just like it is every other day. Even after the semi-crazy weekend, this is who I defer back to. The invisible girl blending into the background. And as much as I try to figure out a way to break out of the redundant pattern, to set my soul free, and let me personality shine, I falter every single time. I equate it to learning how to walk blindfolded in stiletto heels down the side of a mountain. Falling is inevitable. But how many times do I pick myself up and try again is the burning question.

It's exhausting, fighting to become the person you want to be. The person you can envision even when the reality is so far out of reach.

One day, I tell myself, as I contently sip on my piping hot coffee and slip into the empty elevator. I lower my eyelids as the warm, creamy taste of heaven kindles in my chest, chasing away the worry for a millisecond.

It's amazing how something so small can bring you so much comfort.

I'm snapped out of my momentary peace when someone else enters the elevator, the lift shaking slightly as he steps authoritatively inside.

"This one's full." He hits the close button haughtily, guarding the opening like the entrance to Fort Knox.

"Full?" I scan the medium-sized box. It's just me and *him*. I knew who it was the moment he spoke. *Alec-fucking-Prescott. Yay.* So much for my momentary peace.

The double doors slide closed and all the air in the elevator is sucked out like a vacuum.

Fucker.

I press my back against the wall, clutch my coffee cup, and pray the snake doesn't bite. I still can't shake off the way he looked at me Friday night on the balcony of the firm's penthouse. I felt his eyes on me from the inside out. The ground shook beneath me like an earthquake, and for a split second, I thought I was plummeting to my death. It was . . . *an out-of-body experience.* And although it only lasted a few seconds in real time, its impression is permanently branded me. I shiver from the recollection, hoping Alec doesn't catch wind.

I'm not that lucky. He shifts to the side of the elevator, leans on the wall, and stares straight at me. My small shiver morphs into uncomfortable fidgeting. *What is this weirdo's deal?* I push my glasses up my nose and stare back. If he's trying to intimidate me, it's not going to work. At least, I'm not going to let it show that it's working. Tage once told me, "be a rock on the outside even if you feel like a pile of rubble on the inside. It'll help you survive." I have taken that advice to heart, because most of the time, that's what I am. A pile of rubble within. And the only way to protect my fragile self is to confine my feelings in a prison of granite.

Neither of us says a word as we rise toward our office lobby. The whole time, it feels as if Alec is sizing me up. What does he see? Definitely not the girl from the other night. That's probably what he's wondering. How can *she* be the same person? I have news for you, Alec, I have no idea. Most of the time, I struggle to find my identity.

The elevator dings on our floor, but Alec isn't quick to move. I swallow hard, trying not to notice his striking blue eyes or sharp, handsome facial features or thick, wavy black hair styled back perfectly. He's the epitome of temptation when his sour attitude isn't getting in the way.

"Did you have a nice weekend, Miss Paige?" he asks almost as if he's taunting me. As if he knows whatever happened between us on the balcony is still lingering in the air.

"Did you?" I shoot back. The corner of his mouth lifts slightly. It's the only part of the man that moves. And crazily, I feel that small gesture's effect throughout my entire body. It buzzes from my stomach to my groin to my scalp and over again. "I've had better." I do nothing but blink as the doors slide open and he strides out. Leaving me, my coffee, and my confusion behind.

I walk across the lobby and take my seat behind the long, front desk — plop into my seat is more like it. I can't get Alec-fucking-weirdo out of my head.

Lara swivels in her chair next to me. "You look like you've seen a ghost."

"I definitely feel like I just left a freak show." I turn on my computer and take another hefty sip of coffee.

"Did Alec say something strange to you in the elevator?"

"Alec is just strange, plain and simple." I avoid the question entirely.

"Ever." Lara slides across the shiny floor in her chair. "Is there something you're not telling me?"

I swing my head over, my stomach dropping. "Like what?" No one knows about my sordid past. Who my stepfather is or what he did to me. It was buried in a sealed file years ago because I was a minor, and that's where I would like to keep it. The only reminder I have left of those dark days is Tage. He's the last link, and I can't seem to escape him. As much as I want to. As much as I try, he always turns up, no matter how many times I tell him not to. No matter how many times I tell him I don't need him anymore. He's my one solid reminder of that life. Maybe if he goes, all the heartache and pain from that time will go with him.

"Like, is there something going on with you and Alec?" she whispers. I almost throw up in my mouth.

"Something between me and Alec? Eww, no. He's a royal asshole who is all fucking high and mighty. Why would I want anything to do with him?"

"I don't know." Lara shrugs. "Maybe because ever since I dragged you off the balcony Friday night, you've been acting kind of strange."

"Stranger than usual?"

Lara purses her lips. I have her there. "Yes, stranger than usual."

"Like how?"

"Like your head is totally in the clouds, and now, getting off the elevator together, and that look you had on your face. Did he kiss you?" Her voice elevates conspiratorially. "Did he push you up against the wall and say, 'fuck the paperwork'?"

"Ugh." I shove Lara away, and she rolls across the floor, giggling.

"You're an idiot." I slide my glasses back up my nose.

"You love me." She cheerfully types something on her keyboard.

"Sometimes." I roll my eyes. I have a pile of work to do and the last thing I need are distractions. Especially the Alec Prescott kind.

"Speaking of classified relationships, how's yours? Did you and big L have a fun-filled weekend?" Big L is Luke's code name.

"Yes," Lara sighs. "I'm stupidly in love. It's official."

"More importantly, is he?" I peer over at her.

Lara stops all movement and stares off into space. I watch her pretty face, wondering what she's thinking about?

"I think so," she finally answers sweetly. Contently.

I hope so, for your sake.

"Maybe Alec isn't so bad once you get to know him," she considers.

"Maybe I'll never find out because he's completely off limits," I hiss. *Lara, drop it.*

I don't have a chance to get another word in edgewise because an email comes through . . . from *him.*

ALEC: *Can I please see you in my office? Now.*

I GULP. What the fuck does he want now? He usually only tasks out Lara.

"Fuck," I mutter under my breath as I stand and straighten my button-up shirt.

"What is it?" Lara rolls back over to inspect my screen. "Oh?" Her blue eyes widen at the email. "He's bossy."

"It's nothing, I'm sure."

"Un-huh." She rolls back to her computer slowly. I don't know what's worse, Lara confronting me directly or Lara confronting me passive aggressively. I conclude both ways suck.

"Don't sign the paperwork without a lawyer reviewing it first." She winks.

"Enough with the *Fifty Shades* accolades," I huff. The last place I'm going to end up is chained to Alec's bed. And a non-disclosure agreement will never, ever be an option.

I stomp off in the direction of his office, preparing myself for the migraine I'm going to have after this encounter.

With steely resolve, I knock on his door frame. *Let's get this over with.*

"Alec, you wanted to see me?" I elevate my voice politely.

He flicks his crystal blue eyes up from his desk. "Yes. Don't just stand there, come in." His tone isn't exactly rude, but it's not altogether pleasant either. I enter his office. It's comfortably large, with three huge windows looking out over Midtown Manhattan and dark, glossy furnishings that scream high profile. "A case that requires immediate attention has just been passed over to me, and I'll need an extra hand. I have a lot of research to pull together and a small amount of time."

I stand in front of his desk a bit confused. "Doesn't Lara usually assist you on caseloads?"

"She has, in the past. But for this one, I'm requesting you."

"Why?" I blurt out, dumbfounded.

"Why not?" Alec crosses his arms and leans back in his chair.

Because you have barely ever given me the time of day, and when you did, you were a complete and utter asshole. "Don't think you can handle the workload, Miss Paige?"

"I can handle it just fine. What I can't handle are snide remarks and passive-aggressive comments." I cross my arms, mirroring his position.

Alec's eyebrows shoot up, but the rest of his facial features stay in complete control. "If I have offended you recently, I apologize."

Really? Do ya? 'Cause your tone isn't indicating as much. It's still flat and disconnected.

"You just don't have the most pleasant work demeanor sometimes." If I'm going to work with this douche I'm going to put him in his place . . . as professionally as possible.

Now the corners of Alec's lips turn up. I must be amusing him. "Miss Paige, you have quite the set of balls."

My mouth drops. That is completely inappropriate work language.

"Thank you." I pick my jaw up off the floor and smile. Just so he knows.

"I think this arrangement is going to work out just fine." Alec rocks back and forth in his leather office chair.

Let's hope so, for both our sakes. "I'll email you a preliminary to-do list, and then we can reconvene later this afternoon after you review. This case has high visibility and a short window of time. We need to work fast and stay on the ball."

I nod in agreement. The present is about to get that much more complicated.

"Anything else?" I double-check before I leave.

"Yes." Alec picks up his phone. "Thai or Chinese?"

"Excuse me?" I cock my head.

"Thai or Chinese for dinner tonight? We'll be working late." He glances back and forth between his screen and me.

"Um," I swallow thickly. "Chinese. I hate Thai."

"Done." He waves me off.

Dismissed.

I walk down the hallway back toward my desk in a bit of a daze. Working closely with Alec Prescott. Working late with Alec Prescott. Working *all alone* with Alec Prescott.

I plop down into my chair and stare at my computer blankly.

"Well, what did he want?" Lara immediately interrogates me.

"He wants my help with a case." I gaze over at her. "I'm going to be his right hand, apparently." I'm still processing this.

"Oh, really?" Lara's eyes light up. "Stealing one of my junior partners, are you?"

Like she cares. Less work for her, more anxiety for me.

"I didn't do it purposely." I move my mouse around to wake up the screen.

"Sure about that?" She gives me shit.

"One hundred and five percent." Alec's email pops up as my Outlook loads.

I open it to find a thousand links and instructions ten-miles long. *Groan.* "You can totally have him back if you'd like," I offer Alec up on a silver platter.

"Nope. He's your problem now." Lara waves goodbye.

"Fantastic." I drop my chin into my hand and pout.

"Don't look so disappointed. You'll thank me one day." She pops her eyebrows.

"I highly doubt it," I drawl, spiraling into despair. It's only Monday and already it's turning out to be one hell of a week.

I spend all morning combing through Alec's instructions, reading up on our client, the complaint, and a whole host of other legal mumbo jumbo that swallows up hours. This wage discrimination case was just dumped in Alec's lap and now *we* are left scrambling to prepare. He's none-too-happy about it either. Other emails that have landed in my inbox from him have been curt, laced with annoyance, and clearly written in haste.

This is going to be so fun. I'm just the luckiest damn girl in the world.

Our client is being sued by several male employees whose wages where reduced to match their female counterparts. I've assisted on wage discrimination cases before, but this is the first time I've ever seen a situation like this. And apparently, according to the Equal Employment Opportunity Commission's website, reducing the wages of either sex to equalize their pay is a big, fat no-no. Our client looks to be screwed.

"Fucking Christ." Alec shuffles around papers and folders on his desk as I walk into his office for our afternoon meeting. It's three o'clock, I've barely eaten, my eyes hurt, and I have enough caffeine coursing through my veins to power a speed boat. By the looks of it, so does Alec. "Goddamn Tim with his horrific organizational skills and paternity leave. These case files are a disaster." He's clearly frustrated, and I'm clearly amused. I know I shouldn't find satisfaction in his frustration, but I do. Karma's a bitch. I know that all too well.

"I reviewed everything you sent, read up on the laws, researched the company, and set up interview times with complainants starting tomorrow."

"Good. Thank you," he responds distracted, piling up the papers and folders. "We need to review all of these." He picks up the thick pile and gestures to me. "Take a seat and strap in; it's gonna be a bumpy ride."

I juggle the loose papers and overstuffed folders in my arms as I reach over his desk. There is a lot to review. "I tried to organize everything by date so we can get spun up as quickly as possible, but Tim's handwriting is chicken scratch, and I can barely make heads or tails of his damn notes," Alec seethes.

"Good thing you have me, then." I amble over to the round desk on the other side of the room and place the stack down. "I'm fluent in chicken scratch." I push my glasses up my freckled nose.

Alec just blinks at me blankly. I guess he doesn't appreciate my sense of humor. *Sorry, *shrugs* I tried.* "I'll just get started on this." I sit down demurely and begin to sort through the paperwork. I feel like a dumbass. I'm just going to keep my trap shut from now on. No point in trying to establish a courteous working relationship with the man. He clearly isn't interested.

Shithead.

I throw myself into reading. Tim's handwriting isn't that bad. I've seen much worse. I digest all the discovery that's available and read over the depositions. Alec wants a face to face with all the participating parties because he's anal retentive like that and strives to be overly prepared. A trial date is scheduled for next week, but Alec has made it abundantly clear he wants to settle. The opposing side is making settling difficult, though. They want their day in court, and it looks like they want to drag the company's name through the mud while there. Like Alec would ever let that happen. Our client's repu-tation is what's really on the line here. Settling will make everything go away quietly. And according to Tim's notes, the company has been generous with what it's willing to offer. It feels like there is more going on with this case than just the pursuit of fairness.

By six p.m., my eyes feel like they are going to fall out of my head. I can't remember the last time I read so much, and that's saying a lot, because in this job, all I basically do is read. I toss my glasses on the table and rub my tired eyes. There's still an entire stack of papers I have to comb through. We're going to be here all damn night.

"Ready for a break?" Alex asks from across the room.

"Fuck, yes," I expel, then slap my hand over my mouth. *Whoops.* Totally inappropriate work language. Alec grunts. It's more amused than annoyed, which I thank God for. I need this job. I *want* this job. The very last thing I need is Alec getting on my case for not acting professional enough.

"No worries, Miss Paige. Feel free to drop all the F-bombs you want. Lord knows I have been silently cursing my head off. Fucking bullshit of a case." Alec pushes his pile of papers away from him, sending some to the floor. "This shit is open and close. These fuckers just want to drag McKinney's name through the mud. They're wasting everyone's time and money, including their own. Morons." He runs his fingers through his disheveled, dark hair. The move is sort of hot. I shouldn't be noticing that. Nope, not at all.

"Tell me how you really feel," I quip.

"I tell it how it is." He shrugs. "No point beating around the bush."

"Guess not," I agree, even though I'm an expert at avoidance.

Alec's phone buzzes on his desk. He reads the message quickly.

"Dinner has arrived."

Thank God. My stomach has been rumbling for the last forty-five minutes. I barely had time to take three bites of my lunch today.

Several minutes later, a young delivery boy drops off a large brown bag that smells to die for. I know it's just Chinese food, but being on the brink of starvation is making it that much more appetizing.

Alec tips the boy wearing a Giants cap and funky boombox T-shirt as I pull out all the contents of the bag. There are half a dozen little white take-out boxes scattered on the table by the time I'm done.

"It looks like you ordered half the restaurant." I begin to open each one.

"I like variety, and you didn't specify what you wanted to eat. I took a shot in the dark."

"It all looks good to me." I open the chopsticks and attack the chicken and string beans. Yum. I try to interpret the red writing on the container but it's fruitless. I can't read Chinese. "Where did you get this from?" I don't know if I'm just famished or if the food really tastes this damn good.

"I can't give all my secrets away." Alec settles into the chair across from me cockily before picking up his own little box to dive into.

He is so self-important. I internally roll my eyes as I take another bite of the buttery chicken. Fine, keep your stupid, secret —ridiculously amazing — food find to yourself.

I continuously poke at my dinner with the chopsticks, thoughtfully picking and choosing the best pieces to eat. Not a word is spoken for I don't know how long, but when I notice the deafening silence in the room I look up to find Alec staring at me. Intently. Deliberately. Pointedly. He traps me in his icy gaze, the exact same way he did on the balcony, and just like on the balcony, my flesh becomes fevered. It feels foreign, my own skin too tight, tingling with unease. His eyes penetrate me in a way only one other person on this Earth has managed to. *How? Why?* I chew the food in my mouth slowly, concentrating heavily on swallowing. I'm under a spotlight, and I don't know how to react.

Stop looking at me. Break the connection.

But his eyes just linger.

My heart pounds and so does my head, along with some other pulsating places that shall remain nameless. Alec Prescott may be gorgeous, but he's a booming A-hole with a superiority complex I don't want to get anywhere near. Even if he can crawl under my skin with just one look. Just one . . . piercing . . . powerful . . . polarizing look. *Ugh.*

What the fuck is that about? Only one other person in my life has managed to affect me the same way, and look how wonderful that turned out.

I want to shirk under Alec's heavy stare, but I don't. I rally. Staring straight back into his hypnotic blue eyes. Eyes like the Arctic, glacial and blue.

"Han Han." Alec never blinks.

"'Scuse me?"

"The name of the restaurant is Han Han. It's a tiny little place that is one of Chinatown's best kept secrets." He swirls his chopsticks around his box, slowly, thoughtfully, almost like he's trying to seduce me with them.

No, that's crazy. He is not trying to seduce me. Men like him do not seduce women like me. Whoever I may be.

He pulls a small bunch of noodles up out of the box and proceeds to bring them to his mouth all while keeping his eyes pinned on me. I watch silently as his lips part and he slides the long strings into his mouth. He then sucks, drawing in the pasta-like strands. His plump lips becoming glossy from the sauce as the lo mein leisurely disappears.

Holy. Fuck. I know food can be sexy and all, but I'm pretty sure I'm never going to look at a noodle the same way ever again. Alec licks his now grease-kissed lips almost erotically, and I nearly pass out. What the hell is happening here?

Alec then smirks, and something crackles in the air. "I love lo mein." He offers me some noodles with his chopsticks. "Don't you?"

Do I? I don't know. I don't know anything at the moment because it feels as if I entered an alternate reality and my brain function is sluggish.

"It's life." I gulp. *It's life? Oh, dear Lord, someone save me from my own fucking idiocy.*

Alec cracks a smile and then laughs buoyantly. The entertainment on his face and the sound of his amusement is like the sun breaking through dark clouds. It's vibrant and warming and dazzling. For a split second, I see Alec Prescott in a whole different light.

I take his offering, leaning over the table to slurp the lo mein into my mouth. And holy shitballs, it's good.

"Thank you." I cover my mouth while smiling.

"Welcome." He sucks some more through his lips, the smirk staying.

"Chinese really puts you in a good mood," I comment.

"Why, am I usually not?" he asks in all seriousness. I pause, unsure how to respond.

"Um . . ." That impish smile of his returns. "Oh, so you're aware you're cranky."

"Not all the time."

I shoot him a deadpan look.

He stabs his chopsticks into his lo mein. "Okay, not right now."

"I think this is the first time." I purse my lips.

"Not for me."

"Definitely for me."

"You make me sound like I'm a monster walking here." He waves his chopsticks around in the air.

"Up until five minutes ago, I didn't even know you could smile. And the last time we conversed, you weren't exactly . . . *pleasant*."

"How not? We didn't even speak on the balcony."

"Not the balcony. In this very room, before the party. You alluded that I needed more *time* to pull myself together." My tone is snarky.

Alec grunts. "My apologies if I offended you. I was clearly wrong, since you looked stunning at the party." He clears his throat and looks down at his food

Now I know I'm in an alternate reality. *Alec Prescott giving me compliments?* What the hell is in this Chinese food? I steal a glance at my chicken.

"This is a demanding job with high stakes. I can't always afford to be pleasant." He doesn't look at me as he speaks, but his words are amicable.

"A little pleasantry goes a long way," I advise.

Alec flicks his eyes up. "I'll try to remember that."

I nod. If Alec can try, so can I. Maybe this is exactly what we needed, a little one-on-one time to become acquainted with each other.

"Thank you for dinner." I dab my lips with my paper napkin and tidy up my space.

"Leaving?" Alec picks up on my energy.

"It's late. I'm tired, and we need to do it all again tomorrow. If I don't get a good night's sleep, I'll be worthless in the morning."

"Well, we don't want that."

"No." I place my take-out containers in the garbage and then slip my glasses back on. Alec watches my every move, like he's studying me. It makes me feel very exposed. *What is he looking at? What does he see?*

"Thank you again for dinner." I smile sweetly.

"It was my pleasure. It's the least I can do for all your hard work . . . *and for putting up with my crankiness.*" He rips open the top button of his dress shirt.

I find his chagrin cute. "Tomorrow is a new day."

"Yes, it is, Miss Paige." He fiddles with his collar. "Yes, it is . . ."

7

Tage

I WATCH EVERLY EXIT her office building several hours later than usual. I was tempted to go inside and check on her, but I decided against it. She's a big girl now, I continually remind myself. She grew up.

But I still want to protect her.

I do still protect.

I will always protect her.

Even if she doesn't want me to. Even if she hates me. She was one of the reasons I was put on this Earth, and I will always be loyal to her, even if it's from a distance.

I follow her into the subway, staying just far enough away. I trail her like a shadow as she waits for her train, engulfed in her phone, listening to music, hair braided, clothes professional. She's the perfect picture of a normal young woman. It's what I always wanted for her.

Normalcy. It's what I was hell-bent on giving her. Freedom to choose. Freedom to be her.

Freedom, plain and simple.

She hops into a car when the doors slide open, and I follow suit, blending into the mass of people around us. She has no idea I'm only yards away from her. She has no idea, and yet, I want her so badly to notice me.

I just want to peer down into those big green eyes and get lost in them again, the way I used to.

And one day soon, that's exactly what I'll do. Forge a broken bond. A bond *I* broke but plan to piece back together again.

Everly hops off her stop, and I follow behind, tracking her up the stairs back onto the street. The sun has set, so I use the shadows of dusk to conceal myself. A few blocks down from the subway, Ever enters her apartment building. This is as far as I'll go for now. I wait and watch for her lights to turn on. And once they do, I settle into the dark alley diagonal from her bedroom window. Here I stay until she falls asleep. Until the lights in her apartment dim. I pull a piece of paper out of my pocket and slide it through my fingertips. It's tattered and worn from the passing years, but the writing is still legible. It's my last tangible link — to her. It brings me comfort during the darkest of nights. It's my company when I'm lonely, and my reason when I'm lost.

It's my reminder of all the best moments of the past.

8

lec

THE POTENT SMELL of coffee assaults me as I stand in line at the crowded coffee bar. I hate this place. I hate feeling like a sardine squished in a can, fighting for a cup of hot liquid I could send an intern to get. But *she's* here, standing right in front of me, so I'll put up with the annoyances just to be close to her.

This is crazy. It's all so fucking crazy, my attraction to a woman who is totally off limits. Who could cost me my job, and so much more if this little obsession goes too far. But I can't stop thinking about her. She's clouded every thought I've had like a hit from a bong.

A fog of fascination lingering around me. Settling at my feet and following me everywhere.

I eye Everly as she stands there, her brown braids just begging me to pull them. Funny. I never found them appealing before, but working side by side with Everly this past week, I've developed an appreciation for them. Had fantasies about them. About her, dressed in nothing but white lingerie, those naughty braids, and brainiac glasses.

The image makes me shiver. Her smell makes me heady, and her voice hypnotizes me. I am a damn goner, and there's no turning back now.

"I'm sorry, Miss, but your card has been declined," the hipster guy behind the register informs Ever.

"Declined?" She looks down at her credit card. "Can I try one more time?"

He nods. She swipes. Declined again.

"Shit." She flips over the blue card in her hand as if it's going to tell her something.

"Here. Let me," I interject, swiping my card through the machine.

Approved.

"Alec," Everly tries to protest, but it's too late.

"Not a big deal," I interrupt her. "Large coffee with a pump of hazelnut and almond milk, please."

Swipe again. Approved.

"You didn't have to do that." She pushes her glasses up her cute little nose.

"Not a big deal," I repeat. "I know how dependent on caffeine you are."

"This is true." We wait for our morning cup of crack. "But I don't get it. There is plenty of money on my card. It shouldn't have declined."

"It has a chip?" I ask.

"Yes." She bats her eyelashes. *Stop it.*

Sexy.

"They can be temperamental. I would just check your account to make sure everything is copacetic."

"Everything better be copacetic," she gripes. "Stupid credit cards."

The barista calls out her name as she places her coffee cup on the counter.

"Cool name," the young girl comments as Ever claims her cup.

"Thanks." She's always so sweet. Almost sugary. She gives me a fucking toothache.

As we walk to the elevator, worry is evident on Ever's pretty face.

"Don't stress." I touch the crease between her brows. "That's what credit protection is for." She returns a weak smile, but I hate that worry is weighing so heavily on her. The last few days have brought Everly and I closer than I think either of us expected. Once she put me in my place — which was a total fucking turn-on — our working relationship solidified. She may look like a bookworm, but she's anything but. Her tongue is as sharp as her eyes, and her sense of humor is as dark as her hair. She's like a gift you just get to keep unwrapping. Each day, I learn something new, and each day, I'm drawn farther and farther into the magnetizing cosmos that is Everly Paige. "If you want, we can check together, and if anything is off, I'll help you fix it."

"That's very amicable of you, counselor. Would this be pro bono, or am I going to be billed for the hours?" She makes light, even though she's clearly concerned. Do you want to know how you can detect a strong person? It's someone who doesn't fall apart at the first sign of trouble. Someone who keeps their wits, and cool, and sense of humor about them even if there is an impending problem. I learned that quickly about Everly. As soft as she is, she is equally as strong.

She took on every task I threw at her this week and didn't bat an eyelash doing it. She never got flustered, she just endured. I didn't go easy on her, either. We had a job to do, and I made it clear. She made it clear she knew it. She rose to the occasion. On every single front.

"Pro bono," I specify, hoping that will convince her to come to my office. Sneaky. So sneaky.

She considers as the elevator doors ding open. "Well, how can I refuse free legal help?" She cutely takes a sip of her coffee. If I was a betting man, I'd say she's flirting with me with just her eyes.

"You can't." I walk off the elevator all high and mighty. 'Cause, well, let's face it, I am.

Lara spies Everly and me as we walk past the front desk and into the back where the offices are.

"Be back in a bit. Just have to check something out," Everly offers as we disappear through the glass doorway. I don't have to look at Lara to know she speculates something. I overheard her giving Everly an earful about me the other day. They were whispering, and they had no idea I was turning the corner. I stopped short when I heard my name behind the women's room door. Luckily, too. Three more steps, and they would have smacked me right in the face with it. She's convinced something is going on between us. And although nothing is now, her suspicions have merit. Because somehow, some way, I am going to get Everly Paige naked, in my bed, moaning my name. Just you wait. I'm a man of very many talents. And what I want, I get.

I plop down in my office chair and boot up my computer with Everly right next to me. She navigates to her bank's website, and I turn my head when she types in her password. She gasps when her profile pops up.

"Holy shit."

I turn to see her available credit at zero. "Shit is right."

"I've been fucking hacked." She yanks her cell phone out to call the bank as I look over all the charges. Most of them are for high-dollar medical equipment. *How was that not a red flag?*

"Hello, yes." Everly stands up and paces my office as she animatedly explains her predicament to the agent on the other end of the phone. I watch her intently, feeling completely helpless but highly invested. I love watching her. That probably sounds creepy, but I do. I love to investigate all her little facial expressions, and her hand gestures, and her tempting body movements. It's all research. I commit them all to memory, with full intention of using the recon down the line to my advantage. Use it to draw out what she likes. What she loves. What she craves. I'm going to possess her like no other man before and no other man again. She won't even see it coming. That's my plan. Take her by storm. It could be detrimental for both of us, but I threw all my fucks right out the window — or should I say, over the balcony — the night of the party. The night she took *me* by storm. Payback's a bitch and oh, so sweet all at the same time.

"What does a legal secretary need three-thousand dollars' worth of medical equipment for? And shipping it to Guatemala?" she asks exasperated. That does sound bad.

I open my emails and comb through the new ones as Everly gives her bank a piece of her mind. It's adorable.

"Yes." She pinches the bridge of her nose under her glasses. "Yes, thank you." She heaves with a sigh of relief. "How long?" Her eyes pop open. "Up to three weeks?" She turns pale. "Okay. Okay." She glances at me, a myriad of emotions playing on her pretty face. "Thank you." She hangs up, continuing to stand in the middle of the room.

"Good news first?" I ask.

"They identified the purchases as fraud and are going to take care of it."

"And the bad news?"

"It can take up three weeks to reverse the credit." Everly chews on her bottom lip. It's a shiny pink from her lip gloss.

"And that's bad because . . .?"

"It's bad because I basically live off my credit card. I use it to pay for everything, and then pay it all off twice a month."

"When we get paid."

She nods, confirming morosely.

"I have zero cash flow until this is fixed." Worry is overtaking her voice. It's crackling like a snowy TV.

"I can always float you," I offer delicately. "Until this all gets resolved."

"No," Everly objects immediately. Prideful woman.

"Then what are you going to do?"

"I'm not sure, but I'll figure it out. I always do." The last part she mutters under breath, but I hear it. I hear everything, especially when it comes to Everly.

"Well, I'm here . . ." My email updates, and the 'From' address catches my attention. I click the message open and read it in a rush. My heart rate accelerates, and a high of triumph cycles through my system.

"Yes!" I shoot out of my chair, startling the hell out Everly.

"Jesus, what?"

"They want to fucking settle. They caved." I pretend to shoot a basket. *Swish.* "Nothin' but net," I exclaim boastfully.

"Seriously?" Everly tries her best to be excited, but I know her financial problems are freaking her out. I think fast.

"You know what this means, right?"

"We don't have to go to the courthouse?"

"Well, yes that. But also" — my eyes widen with excitement — "we get to celebrate."

"Celebrate?" she questions.

"Yup. Champagne, fancy dinner." *And, if I'm lucky, breakfast, too.*

"Alec . . ." Everly begins to protest.

"Don't even try to talk your way out of it, Miss Paige. You worked as hard as me on this case. You deserve the recognition. And I won't take no for an answer." I throw that last part in there domineeringly. I want her to get the message. For the next few days, she belongs to me, and I'm going to do everything in my power to make her cave. To give in to me. To become all mine.

Everly relents. She received my message loud and clear.

"Okay, fine." A small smile plays on her dewy lips. Victory times two already today, and it's not even nine-thirty yet.

I'm fucking good.

Actually, I'm better than good. I'm a motherfuckin' master.

"Let's get that paperwork prepared so I can send a courier over before lunch."

"Will do."

"And speaking of lunch," I stop Everly before she goes. "Where are *we* going?"

"Today?" she relays, slightly confused.

"Yes, today. Celebration starts as soon as those papers are out the door."

"Shouldn't it start when they're signed?"

I shrug. "Meh. I'm confident in the deal."

"You're the professional." She gives me my well-deserved props. And I do fucking deserve them. I didn't work my ass up from nothing, graduate from Yale at the top of my class, and become the fastest junior partner in this firm's history for nothing. Maybe that's why I come off grouchy all the time. My work is my life, and that's usually how I like it. But even workaholics need something to unwind them. I have habituates, and now, Everly.

"You're right, I am the professional. And he says a celebratory lunch and dinner are on him." I convey, matter-of-factly. "And anything else I feel like throwing in there." Everly cocks her eyebrow, but I cut her to the quick. "Don't question me, Miss Paige."

She rolls her eyes, and I smirk.

"Hot pastrami from Katz's deli."

"'Scuse me?

"That's what I want for lunch. A hot pastrami sandwich from Katz's deli," She returns my matter-of-fact tone.

"That's it?" I curl my lip. "We live in the midst of a culinary mecca, and you want *hot pastrami?*"

"You make it sound so boring."

"It is boring."

"Not when you eat it with me." Everly turns on her heel to leave. "I want sauerkraut and spicy mustard, please." She tosses out her order over her shoulder. "And a Dr. Pepper."

"Anything else?" I ask dryly.

"Just you." We both pause at her flirtatious reply. Something stirs inside me, and the exact same sentiment seems to reflect in Everly's eye. "Your company," she scrambles to clarify, but we both know it's not what she meant. We both know there is something more happening between us. We both know it can be detrimental to our careers, and we both know we just don't care. And now that it is lingering in the atmosphere, there's no turning back. There's no taking it back. There is just moving forward.

9

E verly

"JUST YOU."

I swear I didn't mean to make it sound the way it came out. All sexy, and husky, and *take me right here, right now, right on your fucking office floor*. I mean, Jesus, could I have sounded any more hard-up on the guy? I will admit, though, Alec is the first man in a really long time who actually affects me.

It's more than just a physical attraction, or curiosity about a slightly older, much more successful man. It's something elemental. Something instinctive. Reflexive. Once the veil between us lifted, our connection shifted. Something unexpected happened, and now we are at the precipice of exploring it.

I want to jump, but I also don't. I want to live, but I am terrified of the outcome. My heart is still so tender, but it beats with a fury. I'm confused. I don't know who I am, so how can I be transparent with another person?

With Alec Prescott, no less. He is the epitome of transparent. What you see is what you get. He doesn't pull any punches. He lets you know exactly who he is, and he doesn't care whether you like him or not. That's pretty intimidating, and inspiring.

"Looks like there is a lot going on in that head of yours," Lara comments as she types away.

I just stare at my screen. Maybe I'm more transparent than I think.

"Someone hacked my credit card."

"Oh, shit."

"And Alec wants to take me on a date." Technically, he didn't call it that, but let's just call it what it is.

"Oh, really?" Her interest is explicitly piqued.

"Yes, he wants to take me to dinner, he wants to buy me lunch, he wants to give me all the things." I sigh.

"And that's a problem because?"

"We work together?" It's a rhetorical reply.

"Get over it already."

Yeah, I think that excuse has hit its limit, even if it's the truth and can cost us both our careers.

Probably just mine. I'm expendable.

"Sometimes you have to choose nonsensible over sensible. It's the only way you live. It's what reminds you you're alive. And sometimes, the outcome is favorable."

"What happens when it's not?" I already know the answer to that. I took a risk once. I chose nonsensible over sensible, and all it got me was monumental heartbreak.

"You pick up the pieces and move on." She shrugs.

"You'd be okay with losing everything if things with you and Luke don't work out?" I ask her point-blank.

"Would it suck, yes? Would I be devastated, yes? I love my job. I love my life, but I also love Luke. I'd rather know it didn't work out and learn from my mistakes than wonder what if. That is my biggest fear. . .the 'what ifs'."

I've lived with a thousand what ifs. It's basically all I know. It's the only way I know how to live, but it's not how I want to live.

"You can say no, Ever. Stay home and play your Stories app, like every other night." Her tone is passive, but her message is anything but. "It's your choice. Play a game of life, or actually live one."

Harsh. But she's so right.

I'm tired of pretending to have a life. I actually want one.

I STAND in front of the mirror in a form-fitting, black, off-the-shoulder dress with three-quarter-length bell sleeves. It's understated and elegant and sexy all at the same time. I just ripped the tags off. It's been sitting in my closet for close to a year. I never thought I'd wear it, yet here I am with my hair tied back in a low, sleek ponytail and my nails painted a bright, bold pink.

Alec is taking me to some French-fusion restaurant whose name I can't even pronounce. He said he had to have one of the senior partners pull a string to get a reservation, the wait list is months long. I know I said I want to live, but a date with Alec is intimidating enough. Add all the bells and whistles, and I'm totally out of my element.

The buzzer in my apartment rings, alerting me that Alec is here. I take a deep breath, check myself out one last time, and rush to the front door.

"Yes?" I sing playfully through the intercom.

"Miss Paige, your date has arrived," Alec toys back with me.

I press the button, granting him access into the building.

I'm nervous. So much can go wrong tonight.

But so much can go right, my subconscious hisses. I don't have time to ponder it as my doorbell rings. *He's here,* the little girl's voice from *Poltergeist* rings in my head.

I swing the door open to find Alec dressed in a three-piece, navy blue suit. *Gulp.* He's gorgeous. The color of his suit is making the blue of his irises gleam like a jewel. I have reluctantly admitted that to myself in the past, but tonight I am owning the thought.

He. Is. Gorgeous.

"Wow." His face lights up as he looks me over. He approves. That takes some of the edge off. It probably shouldn't, but it does. I want him to like me. Does that sound pathetic? Probably, but it's the truth. It's been a long time since someone liked me, and I actually liked them back.

My chest pinches from the reminder of the past. But that's just what it is, the past, and that's where it's going to stay. Tonight is all about the present.

"Shall we?" Alec offers me his arm.

"We shall."

10

T age

I watch Everly from afar as she is escorted into a posh restaurant by a man I've never seen before. My blood boils as he puts his hand on the small of her back and walks through the establishment like he owns it, *and her*. They sit at the very end of a large bar that looks into the kitchen of the restaurant. The entire place is all red up-lighting, glossy wooden tables, red cushioned chairs, and gold accents. Dressed the way she is, Everly fits right in to the high-end world. She's beautiful and glowing and happy. She smiles at the douchebag sitting next to her like she doesn't have a care in the world. Ironically, that's exactly how I want her to feel, except I want to be the douchebag sitting next to her. It's supposed to be me. It was always meant to be me.

I know I should just leave her alone, but I can't. I have wanted her to move on with her life for so long, and now that she obviously is, I can't bear the thought of her being with anyone except me.

My feet move faster than my mind. Slipping into the restaurant undetected, I make myself invisible among the bar crowd. The place is packed, with a line at the door. I steal a glance at a plate being carried by a waiter. Two stalks of asparagus with black stuff sprinkled across the top. That's the whole dish. Seems a bit anticlimactic to me. Disappointing, if I'm being blunt. I move around the perimeter of the restaurant until her face is in clear view. It takes her a while to notice me, but when she does, the alarm of my presence is evident in her stare. Our gazes catch, then lock, her green eyes trapped by mine. It's only for a few precious seconds, then I disappear. I wanted to send a message, and by the looks of it, she received it.

I'm always watching. I'm never far.

You'll always, one way or another, belong to me.

11

---

lec

EVERLY LOOKS like she just saw a ghost.

"Everly? Ever, are you all right?"

"Hmm?" She blinks rapidly. "Yes, of course."

"You sure? 'Cause it looked like something spooked you."

"No, not at all." She smiles, and the woman I was just conversing with returns. "I'm here. With you."

"Right where you want to be?" I lean in closer to her.

"Yes." She bites her lip. Gone is the demure librarian from work, in her place is a vixen who captivates my entire attention. It's amazing how she can be two entirely different people in one enticing body. She's like Diana Prince and Wonder Woman or Linda Lee Danvers and Supergirl. Two completely different alter egos behind the same pair of gorgeous green eyes.

"It's where I want to be, too. With you." I'm not going to waste a second beating around the bush. I want Everly, and I want to make it crystal clear. If the last week has affirmed anything, it's that my attraction to this woman is real and warranted and not fizzling out anytime soon. I breathed her in, and now she's a part of me. In my bloodstream, moving my cells, causing my heart to beat.

Our celebratory dinner consists of several bottles of prosecco and several tapas plates, including green asparagus mimosa with imperial caviar and wasabi whipped cream, roasted baby artichoke with a chickpea emulsion, and spicy duck with kumquat confits. If it sounds showy, ostentatious, and pretentious, that's because it is. I want to impress Everly. I want to show her how good life can be. I consist of upscale taste and meager beginnings. For some reason, I feel like Everly can relate.

By the third bottle of bubbly, our bellies are full and our heads are light. Everly is resting her hand on my thigh while I caress the bare skin on her shoulder. She knew what the hell she was doing when she picked out this dress.

"I don't want this night to end," I murmur in her ear as the minutes tick away. It's nearly midnight, and the restaurant is thinning out. The kitchen is closed, and the bartenders are relaying last call.

Everly's eyes widen, but not in hesitation or fear, more in excitement. In a way that communicates she feels the same.

"So, let's not let it." She swipes her thumb back and forth over the material of my dress pants, sending a shock of exhilaration coursing through my body. I want her to touch me so much more. So much more intimately.

"We can go back to my place." I run my lips over the curve of her neck, the temperature in the room rapidly rising.

"I'd like that." I can almost hear the rapid acceleration of her heartbeat as she agrees. We are stepping over a serious threshold. Both our careers hang in the balance. Moving our relationship to the next level isn't anything to fool with. But we are both consenting adults, whose attraction is apparent to more than just us. The few people left in the room notice it, too.

I pay the check and lead Everly away. I hail a cab and verbally toss my address to the driver. We aren't very far but nowhere near close enough to walk. The driver speeds through the streets of Manhattan, but the only thing I can concentrate on is the woman sitting beside me. Confined in the back seat, there's no excuse not to touch her. No excuse not to pull her close and take advantage of the small space. I want to kiss her. The urge has a life of its own. I've been fantasizing about those plump, pouty lips for days, and I'm finally ready to make my dreams a reality.

I inhale her spicy-sweet scent as I touch her reverently. I want her to feel how much I want her. How much I respect her. How tender I can be.

"Alec," she sighs as I run the tip of my nose up her neck. God, that sound. My name spilling from her mouth, it causes an uproar inside me. I want to hear it again and again, all fucking night long. While I pin her down, while she rides me, while I take her from behind. I cup her cheek with one hand and trap her face an inch away from mine. We both breathe heavily from the anticipation of what's to come. I move my mouth fractionally closer to hers, and her lips part. She wants me. Wants this. But just before I close the distance, she places her palm on my chest.

"Alec?"

I pause all movement. I thought she wanted this. I read the signs.

Everly searches for something in my eyes. "What is it?"

"Can I ask you something?" She doesn't move. She doesn't pull away or push me away. She keeps us close.

"Anything."

She swallows anxiously. "Who do you see when you look at me?"

I know the answer immediately. I know exactly who I see when I look at Everly.

"I see someone" — I caress my thumb across her cheek — "who is so much more than whom she portrays herself to be." And it's the

God's honest truth. Her exterior might be mild-mannered, but there is a passionate wind blowing beneath the surface.

Her eyes become glassy as she gazes at me. It's only for a short moment, but it is a profound one. Any space left between us evaporates as Everly crushes her mouth to mine. The kiss escalates in an instant, becoming everything I'd imagined it would be. Hot, needy, hungry, thrilling. A glorification of lust and a facilitation of emotion.

I fuse our lips, darting and rolling my tongue until neither of us can breathe. I feel like the Hulk growing in the small backseat of the taxi cab. I need to get out. I need to expand. My hormones are raging, and the only antidote that can sate the animalistic creature is Everly's body.

The elevator ride up to my apartment is virtually a blur as my entire concentration is consumed by the spellbinding brunette allowing me to run my hands all over her body.

The entryway is dark as I push open the door and we stumble into the apartment. I'll give Ever the two-cent tour of the place tomorrow. Right now, all she needs to worry about is where the bedroom is.

With our lips molded together, I walk her into the shadowy room, the skyscape of Manhattan glittering through the picture windows.

As much as I want to rip her clothes off and throw her on the bed, I equally as much want to take my time exploring her curves. Exploring all her secret places and sensitive spots.

I'm a man tearing in two. My wants clashing like Titans.

Pumping the brakes, I put some separation between us. Just enough to keep Everly in my grasp but also enough to admire the woman standing before me.

Her cheeks are pink, her eyes are dilated, and there is a small, sheepish smile playing on her lips. God, she's beautiful, and I don't even think she realizes. I didn't realize, and I'll be the first to admit I was a fucking asshole for it.

But not anymore. I know what I have now. What I refuse to let go of.

I sit on the edge of my bed and stare up at the gift the universe has offered me. Running my hands gradually along Everly's curves, she places her palms on my neck. A pivotal moment passes between us. It feels like a day of reckoning. I am going to show Everly how much I want her. How my misjudgment and indiscretions of the past are no longer.

"I have been thinking about you all goddamn day." I tighten my grip on her hips.

"Good, because I've been thinking about you, too." Her voice is faint and so fucking alluring.

"Oh, yeah? What were you thinking about?"

"This. Right here, right now. If we were ever going to get to this point."

"Did you have doubts?"

"Maybe a few," she confesses.

"I know I'm not always the most tolerable person. Or the nicest, or warmest, but being with you, I feel different." I drop my head and stare into the blackness of her dress. "You make me want to be different." It's my turn to confess. For as long as I can remember, work has been my main priority. To strive professionally and reach an elevated level of success, and up until now, I have excelled. But Everly has made me realize there is so much more to life than just work, or money, or status. There's intimacy and companionship and affection. My job has always been my first love, but now there's room for another, and she's standing right in front of me.

I feel Everly's sweet touch on my cheek. "You make me want to be different, too." I lift my head to gaze up at her face. "I have avoided *life* for so long, but I don't want to do that anymore. I don't want to be alone or hide. I want . . . *more*." She struggles to find the right word.

"With me, you can have more." That's all I want, to give her more.

With a bright smile, she asks, "So, what are we waiting for?"

I mirror her facial expression. "Not a damn thing." *Life* starts right fucking now.

Inhaling a collective breath, Everly reaches around and unzips her dress. The oxygen in the room thins as she seductively peels the clingy material from her body. I don't even think she's trying to be sexy — she just is.

Once it falls to the ground, I breathe in the crackling atmosphere. It gets me higher than THC.

All self-control is gone after that. My hands explore her bare body as my tongue puts on a show, tracing the curve of her abdomen, circling around her belly button, and moving north to her breasts. She isn't wearing a bra, so I have free rein to explore. Massaging both of her firm, round breasts at the same time, I lick and suck on her nipples slowly, giving each one the attention it deserves. They pebble against my tongue, spurring me to nip and tug and suck even harder. Everly responds in the most arousing way, moaning and sighing, running her fingers through my hair over and over as I lavish her.

"God, that feels good," she expels.

"Just wait," I promise her. I'm just getting started. Tugging at the string of her underwear, I increase the pressure with my mouth, biting the flesh of her perky breasts, close to leaving a mark.

I want to mark her. I want her and the world to know she's all mine.

"Alec." My name spilling from her lips has my balls tingling. I need more. I need to get closer.

I urge Everly onto the mattress, pinning her beneath me as I attack her mouth. The kiss is brutal and hot, our tongues ravenous as they duel against each other.

Pressing my pelvis against her, my erection howls in pain. Fucking Christ, I want the woman unlike any before her. It's a force.

The sounds of lust echoing through my bedroom are acoustical. A melody of need climbing to a crescendo.

Kneeling above Everly, she frantically helps me unbutton my dress shirt and then my pants. Our fingers tangling in the rush. Once my shirt is a distant memory and my pants are hanging around my waist, I latch my lips onto her collarbone and suck before moving down her body. There's only one spot I want to be. One spot I want to indulge in, smother myself with, overdose on.

Right as I reach the line of her panties, I slow to a crawl, prolonging the inevitable collision. I peel the black silk away gradually, gliding the strings and scrap of material covering the slit of her pussy over her hip bones, and away. The smell of her is heavenly, sweet and spicy, like a piece of candied ginger.

"Spread your legs," I growl low in my throat. I'm a gluttonous animal about to feast.

The small, apprehensive squeak that escapes her has me on high alert. I love that she's breaking down. That she's allowing herself to trust me. I could spend the rest of eternity between Everly's thighs. Just the mere scent of her has me salivating.

With my eyes pinned on her face, I lick her clit lightly, taking my time to savor her taste. Her eyes are glued shut, and she's clutching the pillow on both sides of her head. She's sexy as all hell, wound-up tight.

I glide the tip of my tongue through her folds with more pressure this time, and she moans.

Yes. It's the exact reaction I want.

I don't want her to come, but I do want her wet, so I continue my leisurely ministrations, pushing her thighs wider as I slide my tongue deeper and deeper.

"Oh, God, Alec." She bows her body and mewls as I swipe my tongue up and down, teasing her clit and then her entrance. Over and over, I follow the same path until she's panting. Until her arousal is soaking her pussy and my mouth. She's so ready. So wanton. And I'm exactly the same. I need to be inside her. I need to feel her come.

With one last firm tug on her clit, I unlatch my mouth and move back up her body. Her chest is heaving, and her abdomen is quaking. She's so close.

"Are you on the pill or do I need a condom?" I ask between kisses deeper than the sea.

"Pill," she huffs, latching her arms around my neck.

Thank you, Jesus.

Shedding my pants and underwear, there is nothing left standing between us.

"I want to watch you come. I want you to ride me until neither of us can breathe." I roll her over and position her on top of me. There's hesitation on her pretty face, but this is the way I want it. "Trust me." I caress her cheek, putting her at ease. "You're so fucking beautiful, I want to see everything." I feel her skin actually heat under my touch.

Everly exhales heavily, giving in to my demand. I know she's strong enough to handle anything I throw at her. It's a huge part of her appeal.

Straddling me, her naked form illuminates in the light filtering in from the city buildings.

"I want to feel you, baby." I rub encouraging circles into her thighs with the pads of my thumbs.

Everly leans down to kiss me, lifting her hips to allow me access. We're both amped up, the arousal coursing through our veins like the stimulant it is.

"Slow," I rasp as I guide the head of my erection to her entrance.

"Okay," she whispers as she plants her hands on my chest for support and inches down deliberately. Millimeter by millimeter, engulfing my cock in her soaking wet heat.

I groan in ecstasy, my eyes closed, my head thrown back as the tightness of her pussy squeezes and massages the entire length of my throbbing shaft.

So. Fucking. Good.

Once she's fully seated on top of me, and my erection is snug inside of her, I grip her hips and hold her there. Steadying her in place so my cock can jerk, adjusting to the feel of her constricting muscles.

Slow, slow, slow, I chant to myself. The minute we become crazed, it will be over. I won't be able to control myself.

"Move. God, baby, move slow," I direct, sounding like a delirious man.

Why don't we just fucking face facts? *I am.*

I'm deliriously infatuated with the woman who is presently riding me. Who's moving her hips up and down so painstakingly slow it's making me as mad as a hatter.

I watch Everly's face, entranced, studying each and every expression the measured stimulation brings forth.

Her lips part and her brows crease every time she slides downward. Her body bows and her voice squeaks every time I thrust upward. Round and round we continuously go, indulging in the languid pleasure while both inwardly pleading for more.

"Alec." Everly digs her nails into my skin as her muscles contract. She's getting close, fighting the impending end.

I tense my body, drilling my fingertips into her hips as I guide her up and down.

"Alec, please." She drops her head back, her nipples sharper than nails. "I need more."

"You want to come all over me?" I goad her.

"Fuck, yes." She rocks a little harder, and my nerve endings light up. "I want to so bad." Her limbs quiver.

"Just like this." I only allow her a bit more friction. "I want to watch. I want to see everything".

She continues to pump her hips at a medium speed, her cheeks becoming flushed, and her inner walls pounding commandingly.

"Oh, fuck," she croons agitatedly as the sensations take hold. "Oh, fuck. Oh, fuck. Oh, fuck," she cries while riding me, the rush of her orgasm dragging us both under. She's a spectacular sight above me, her tits bouncing in the moonlight as she owns her pleasure.

The peak of her climax has me tearing in two. The blissfully torturous pulsing, shooting, and flashing sensations disintegrates my resolve. I can't hold back any longer. I flip Everly onto her back, and in a blind rage, I pull out, jerking my cock until I'm splashing cum all over her body. Coating her stomach and chest in violent sprays of arousal, officially marking what I'm claiming as mine.

Holy fuck. I suck in air like a vacuum as stars dance in my vision.

There's nothing after that, just white noise crackling through the darkness of my bedroom and two warm bodies molded together as one.

12

E verly

I CRACK my eyes open and am blinded by sunlight.

My body is tired and so is my mind. The effects of last night slowly creep over me as I remember vivid details of Alec and each one of our several sexual encounters.

"Good morning, Sleeping Beauty." I roll my head over on the pillow to find Alec propped up on one arm, staring at me.

I smile. "Good morning."

"I take it you slept well?"

"What gave it away?"

"Your snoring."

"I don't snore." I slap his chest with the back of my hand.

"Okay, I wouldn't technically call it snoring, but you do make sounds."

"Sounds?"

"Mmm-hmm." He runs one fingertip along my hairline. "You squeak."

"Squeak?"

"And whimper."

"Whimper?" I frown.

"It's adorable." He smiles.

"Seriously?"

"Seriously."

"If you say so."

"I do." He's adamant. That arrogant attitude is so the Alec I know. "Your roots are red." He's inspecting me.

"I'm a natural redhead. I dye my hair brown."

"Ah. That makes a lot of sense." He walks his fingertips down my forehead to my nose. "The freckles."

"Yes," I confirm. "They are even more prominent in the sun."

"I'd like to see that."

"Why? I hate them. They're ugly."

"I love them. They're beautiful," Alec contests. "They become you."

"My mother used to say that." I grimace. It's one of the few nice things she ever said to me.

"Well, she was right." His hand travels down my naked body. "Where are your parents?"

"Gone." My one-word answer causes him to stop.

"Dead?" he asks delicately.

I wish.

"No, just gone. I haven't had a relationship with them in a very long time," I reluctantly share. My parents are never a joyous subject for me.

"I'm sorry to hear that." His hand picks up where it left off, moving south down my torso.

"Don't be. I'm better off without them. Trust me."

"I do trust you." His movements stop a few dangerous inches below my belly button. I look up into his blue eyes. *What now?*

"I have a good relationship with my parents." He backtracks, circling my navel.

"That's good."

"They're not my biological parents. They adopted me when I was two months old."

"Oh?"

Alec nods as he continues to orbit my belly button. "They barely had two nickels to rub together, but they took me in. I didn't have money growing up, but I did have them."

"You're lucky."

"I am." He stares into my eyes. "For the second time in my life, an amazing person gave me a chance."

There is no stopping the blush that creeps over my cheeks. "I'm not amazing."

"You are, and you don't even know it." His hand starts to move south. "You asked me who I saw when I looked at you." He caresses my clit, and I shiver. "I see someone amazing. And you'll never be able to convince me otherwise." Alec sinks one sneaky finger into my entrance, and I fall apart. His touch is blindsiding.

I sigh as he fingers me, his words echoing in my ear.

"You have no idea how good that feels." I melt into the pillowy mattress.

"I think I have an idea." He sucks on my neck as he works his hand, switching gears from slow to fast, and then slow again.

It's remarkable how quickly he's learned to read my body. One night together and he already knows which perfect buttons to push.

Shoving the black covers away, he exposes our bare forms. "Will you let me watch you come?"

"You enjoy doing that." I drop my knees and sigh.

"Very fucking much." He bites my neck, as he slides two fingers inside me this time. "It's an addiction."

"I can live with that." I jerk when he caresses my g-spot. Fuck, I'm going to explode faster than a time bomb.

"Put your hands over your head." Alec's voice is so thick with desire it's barely recognizable.

I do as he requests, elongating my body as seductively as possible.

"Fuck, yes." He draws one nipple into his mouth, stacking the sensations. I want to give him what he wants, so I hand myself over and get lost in his touch. In the feel of his mouth and excitement he brings forth. Before long, my limbs are tingling and so is my pussy. I moan and writhe, playing right into his hands. Living the part he's desperate to see play out.

The hormonal commotion fluttering inside me builds until it's no longer containable. Every muscle in my body tenses, the ones clamped around Alec's fingers throbbing.

He holds my wrists down as I come, forcing the sensations to gravitate to one central location — right between my legs. I let out a wail as my hips jerk on the bed. It's feels so fucking good. So fucking freeing and maddening and cathartic all at the same time. It's been so long since anyone has touched me like this. Since I've allowed anyone in.

"Alec," I pant. "God, Alec." I'm disoriented as I float down from my high.

"I'm right here," he hums in my ear. "I don't think I'll ever get tired of watching that."

"You enjoyed the show?" I toy with him.

"Immensely." He takes one of my hands and guides it to his erection. He's rock fucking hard and ready to go.

"What do you want?" I ask seductively.

"These." He outlines my lips. "Wrapped around my cock."

"I can do that." I suck on his finger the same way I'm going to suck on his cock.

"Mmm," he grunts as I push myself up and kiss my way down his body.

Alec's chest is smooth, but he has a sexy trail of hair right below his navel. I love it. It's soft to the touch and utterly masculine.

He stretches out on the mattress in clear anticipation. I swirl my tongue around the head of his erection, and he expels a low, throaty growl. I love his reaction. I love that it's a genuine reaction to me.

I swallow his cock as deeply as I can, spurring him to tense. He's receptive to my mouth, moaning when I suck and growling when I pull away.

These acts are so much more than just physical. There's a connection between us. A connection like I've only felt with one other man. That scares me on so many levels given our history, but I continuously remind myself Alec is not Tage. The situations are completely different. This time, I'm free.

"Ever." Alec grabs my disheveled ponytail and yanks. "Fuck, I'm gonna come." His jaw clenches, his thigh muscles quivering as I continue to suck and jerk until my palm and his shaft are soaked with my saliva and spurts of cum are exploding in my mouth.

It's as satisfying to make him come as it is to come myself.

"Jesus, woman." Alec pulls me into his arms and crushes me against his chest. "I may never let you leave this bed."

I giggle. "You'll have to wait on me hand and foot."

"I can live with that." He chuckles.

"Well, if that's the new arrangement, can you start by bringing me coffee?"

"How about we start by swinging by your apartment so you can change and I can take you to lunch? After that, I'll confine you to the bed."

"Kidnapping me for the weekend, are you?"

"Absolutely." Alec cozies up beside me. "I want this body naked for as long as possible."

"I think we can arrange that." I dot a kiss on his lips, then his jawbone, then his neck.

"Keep that up and we'll never make it to lunch," he growls.

AFTER A QUICK PIT stop at my place to change, shower, and feed

Denali, Alec and I ended up at a casual little lunch place by the Garment District. It's packed, of course, but we scored a booth and a halfway-decent waiter.

I obviously worked up a serious appetite last night because I found myself ordering fried chicken and cheddar cheese waffles. Not a usual meal for me, but they looked so good I couldn't pass it up. Alec went with a short rib sandwich and crispy brussels sprouts.

We sip on coffee and ice water as we wait for our food. His fingers find mine across the table, and they do a little intimate dance as we enjoy the feel of each other.

Alec's presence is as commanding out of the office as it is in it. Except he's much less intimidating in a light blue T-shirt and faded jeans. This morning, he looks boyish and buoyant. It's easy to forget just how young he really is compared to most of the other junior partners.

"What made you want to become a lawyer?" I ask.

"It was challenging. It allowed me multiple opportunities to grow professionally, and it paid well."

"It wasn't because you wanted to help people?"

"Yeah, that, too." Alec shrugs.

I shake my head and laugh.

"What? I am a very left side of the brain person. I analyze everything."

"I've noticed."

"What else have you noticed?" Alec leans over and flirts.

Okay, I'll play. I lean forward, as well, so our faces are only inches apart. "I've noticed that even though you come off matter-of-fact and cool, underneath that rigid exterior is a man who is funny and generous and kind."

"Oh, really?"

"Yes," I confirm.

"Anything else?" We continue to move closer, a force of nature taking control of our bodies.

"There's one more thing," I whisper.

"What's that?" His tone matches mine.

"You're a great kisser." Our lips touch, but our intimate interaction is disrupted by a loud, irritated cough.

We break apart, and when I look up, I swear I turn pale. Tage is standing before us, arms crossed, stare daunting.

What the fuck is he doing here?

"We aren't getting up any time soon, man," Alec brushes him off, of course having no idea who the man is.

Tage slides his daunting hazel eyes over to Alec. "That's cool, *man.* I'll just join you." He slips into the booth beside me.

Alec is appalled.

"Listen, asshole—" Alec's signature short temper flares.

"It's okay," I intervene before a fist fight breaks outs. "I know him. He's sort of a friend." I glare at Tage. I don't know what game he's playing, but it's going to end right now. First, he stalks me on my date last night, and now this?

"What are you doing here?" I cut to the chase.

"That's not a very nice tone to take, Everly." Tage reaches for my water and takes a sip. "Aren't you going to introduce me to your friend? I love meeting new friends of yours."

I look past Tage at the exposed brick wall to collect my bearings. This is so not cool.

I huff. "Tage, this is Alec. Alec, Tage," I make the quick introduction.

Alec looks as unhappy about our unwelcomed lunch guest as I am.

"Pleasure." Tage reaches out his hand.

Alec looks at it like it's diseased. He is the last person Tage is going to walk all over. Tage pulls his hand back, seemingly not bothered at all. He's good at that. The brush-off.

"So, how did you two meet?" He's being beyond obnoxious.

"Work," I answer curtly.

His attention jumps between Alec and me. "Isn't there a strict rule about coworkers dating at your firm? It's a no-no, right?"

I can almost see blue flames shooting out of Alec's eyes. "You're not part of our firm, so the on-goings within it mean nothing to you."

Tage grunts. "See, *Alec*, that's where you're wrong. When it involves Everly, it will always mean something to me. And if you're putting her career in jeopardy just to get your rocks off, I definitely have something to say about that." Tage straight up threatens him.

"Tage," I hiss. I don't know what's gotten into him. The man has drifted in and out of my life like a ghost the past eight years, and he chooses *now* to manifest. He chooses *now* to suddenly take an active interest? "I think it's time for you to go."

"I second that," Alec spits.

The waiter chooses to drop our food at that very moment. The smell makes me hungry and turns my stomach all at the same time.

"I'll let you two eat. Looks delicious." Tage steals a French fry from Alec's plate. "I'll be watching you." He leans over as he stands, getting in Alec's face.

"Watch, learn, and be envious." Alec isn't intimidated in the least. That hard exterior runs straight to the core. Too bad Tage has one to match.

We watch him saunter out of the small restaurant, and once he's gone, Alec zeroes in on me.

"Explain."

I want to slink under the table in embarrassment.

"I'm sorry, I don't know what got into him."

"Who is he?"

"A very old acquaintance." I don't even want to use the word friend at the moment.

"And you were acquainted how?" Alec never pulls a punch.

I don't want to launch into my past. It's so fucking messy. And it's something I'm not even supposed to talk about. That was the deal.

"Remember how I told you my parents were gone?"

"Yes."

"Well, Tage sort of stepped in and took care of me during a very tumultuous time in my life. He's sort of like the big brother I never wanted."

No, I never saw him as a big brother. He was my first love and an epic heartbreak. Being in his presence is physically taxing. My soul still calls out to him, but he made it clear we could never have a life together. *We were never meant to be together.* It's taken me years to come to terms with that, and truth be told, today, for the first time, my emotions didn't shatter when I saw him. I think Alec is filling the void inside of me faster than I could have imagined. Than I could have anticipated. He's the new beginning I so desperately needed.

And I like it. I want it. I want him. "He's no one you have to worry about. I promise. He's just protective." I reach across the table and grab his hand.

"He doesn't need to be protective anymore. You have me now." Alec squeezes my fingers. The gesture makes my heart swell.

"I'll make sure he gets the message." I smile. "Loud and clear."

lec

OVERPROTECTIVE IS an understatement when it comes to Everly. The woman has completely invaded. She's all I think about when we're not together, dream about when she's not in my bed, taste when I'm not kissing her.

It's been one solid week we've officially been 'dating', and my life feels complete. I have come to realize she's the piece I didn't even know was missing.

"Alec Prescott?" A woman's voice beckons me on the street as I reach for the door handle of a black sedan.

I look over to find a nice-looking, middle-aged woman in a white suit standing on the sidewalk next to me.

"Yes?"

Her lips twist up.

"Mr. Prescott, you've recently become somewhat of an interest to several of my associates."

"And which associates might that be?" I ask suspiciously.

The woman just smiles wryly. "Those names will be revealed in due time. For now, I have a proposition for you."

"Do you now?"

"I do."

"I don't have time for propositions. If you need a lawyer, call my office. The secretary will set you up." I jerk open the door.

"Yes, it's the secretary they're most intrigued with."

That stops me dead in my tracks.

"What about her?"

The droll expression never leaves the woman's face. "I'll be in touch, Mr. Prescott."

A moment later, a red Porsche with tinted windows pulls up next to the Town Car. The woman steps off the sidewalk in a rush and disappears inside. It speeds off into traffic after that.

I'm left bewildered. What the fuck was that shit about? I replay the encounter over and over *"It's the secretary they're most intrigued with."*

An ominous feeling stabs me in the gut.

Could Everly be in trouble? It may explain the weirdo who joined us for lunch last week. I can't image her tangled up in anything more dangerous than Christmas ribbon. . . or the sheets in my bed.

It's nearly three by the time I get back to the office. I have been wrapped up in court proceedings all day and am done with this week. I just want some peace, and I want Everly.

Naked, preferably.

The elevator doors ding open, and like usual, Ever and Lara are sitting behind the long, sleek, wooden desk that guards the doors to the entrance of the firm. They're like gatekeepers — no one gets in or out without them knowing.

"Ladies," I acknowledge them as I walk past. Lara smiles as she types away at her computer, but Everly's eyes catch mine. They're encased behind her black-rimmed glasses. A reel of dirty images suddenly invades me. I stop short. "Miss Paige, would you be available to work late tonight? I have a mountain of discovery I need to comb through."

Lara's head snaps up as Everly answers. "Tonight? But it's Friday? Don't you have a hot date?" She's totally toying with me.

"I do." I confirm. "But I'll make it up to her . . . if she'll let me."

Innuendo is flying all over the room. Lara doesn't miss a beat. She knows exactly what's up. Her expression says it all. So does mine, and so does Everly's. If Luke was standing next to me, we would be a double duo of defiance.

"I'll stay if I must," she sighs.

"You must," I smirk, opening the glass door.

Back to my office I go.

EVERLY AND I spend several hours reading over case documents. I wasn't kidding when I said I had a mountain of discovery to comb though. We ordered Chinese and ate while the sun set behind the skyscrapers. New York is a magical city. So much life, so much diversity, and yet, when you look for it, so much peace.

By nightfall, we are the only ones left in the office. It's quiet, save for the shuffling of papers here and there. We haven't been alone like this in my office since the case. There's been no need. My workload doesn't coincide with hers. If things were done the proper way, it would be Lara sitting here with me.

But who cares about proper? Right now, the only thing I care about is spreading Everly out over my desk.

"Ready for a break?" I ask from across the room.

"God, yes." She shoves her glasses up onto her head and rubs her eyes.

I pat my lap, beckoning her to me.

She automatically glances out the office window, but there's no one here. "Shut the blinds if it makes you feel better."

After a beat, she gets up and does just that. She locks the door, too. Now we're gettin' somewhere.

She crosses the room to where I'm sitting and props herself up on my desk directly in front of me. I was thinking more like she'd sit on my lap, but this is good, too. She's wearing a black-and-white striped silk shirt and a tight-ass pencil skirt. She has a bibliophile sex appeal.

"Hey, baby." I rub my palms along her thighs.

"Hey, yourself." She rewards me with a warm, sensual smile.

"I have been thinking about you all day."

"Oh, yeah?" Everly reaches out and places her hands on my shoulders. "What *exactly* were you thinking about?"

"I was thinking about you, just like this." I roll my chair closer so she's forced to spread her legs, the hem of her skirt hiking sky-high. "All mine, to do with what I please."

"And what do you please?" She widens her thighs enticingly.

"Seems the same thing you do." I lick my lips when I get a peek of her pink panties.

"I definitely wouldn't stop you." Everly leans back, supporting her weight on her hands.

The savage inside me snarls. My woman, my property, my domain.

Just as I reach under her skirt to rip off her underwear, I'm struck with a recollection. The encounter with the woman from earlier today.

"Alec?" Everly whispers my name. Her hand placed gently on my cheek. "You okay?"

I slide my eyes up to hers. They're round, and soft, and hazy with desire.

"Ever," I force out. "You'd tell me if you were in trouble, right?"

She blinks, confused. Her eyelashes fluttering a mile a minute. "Of course, I would. Why?"

I search her expression for any untruth. For an inclination that she's lying to me.

But all I see is sincerity. All I feel is sincerity.

"I just want you to know that you can confide in me. That you can tell me anything."

The skin between her eyebrows dimples. I love it when it does that. It's fucking adorable.

"I trust you, Alec. I'm not in any trouble. I promise." She looks me dead in the eyes. "For the first time, in a long time, I'm in a really good place."

"So am I." I melt under her stare. She has no idea the affect she has on me. The power she has over me. I see so much when I look at Everly. Time, space, and a future I never dreamed of having.

We lean in at the same time, as if the universe is urging us to kiss. It's a slow, soft roll of our tongues and a sweet, succulent suck of our lips. My hands travel back to their original destination, under Ever's skirt. I peel her panties down her thighs and dispose of them on the floor. Before I push her back, positioning her exactly the way I want—splayed out on top of my desk—I slide her glasses down to her nose. "I want you wearing these." Smart is fucking sexy. Hooking my arms under her thighs, I drop my head and indulge in dessert. Licking up the sugary taste of pussy I can't seem to get enough of.

This moment, by far, is the hottest of my life. Never in a million years did I picture myself defiling my desk, but when you have a woman as hypnotic as Everly right at your fingertips, you take full advantage.

"Mmmm, Alec," she moans, detached from reality as I circle my tongue and suck on her clit. I take my time, enjoying the feel of her soft flesh against my mouth and sticky moisture coating both our lips.

Dipping the tip of my tongue into her entrance, I begin a figure eight of pleasure, moving up and around her inflamed nub and then back down again. In and out, up and down, I slowly drive her to the brink of madness.

"Alec!" She crunches up and cries as her body spasms.

I don't relent, I want her to fall to pieces. I want her squirming and writhing, then screaming in ecstasy as she rains arousal all over my tongue.

"Oh, God, oh, fuck," she pants, pulling on my hair. My cock strains painfully in reaction to her. I love it when she comes. I love it when she's free. It's the ultimate fucking turn-on.

"Ah!" Her voice pitches when she breaks, thrusting her hips frantically against my face as she climaxes.

Everly collapses once the seizure passes. All thought and reason have been completely wiped clean from my mind as I stand and unbutton my pants. There is only one thing driving me—the need to be inside Everly.

Once my erection is free, I slam into Ever like the savage I've become. I can't even control it. My need has completely taken over.

"Alec." She sits up and tenses as I blindly thrust again and again, my orgasm amassing like an army prepared for battle.

"You'll never know how good you fucking feel." I grab her hair as the buildup becomes volatile.

Her pussy saturates me, my cock swells, my tailbone tingles, and then there's full-on destruction. I bite down on Everly's neck as I come, the sensations tossing me around like a rag doll in a raging sea.

I heave with Ever still in my arms. My head is light, and my limbs are jelly, but the satisfaction spreading throughout my body like warm honey is a high unlike any other.

This fucking woman and what she can do to me.

"Let's go home."

"Can't we just sleep here?" she mumbles lazily.

"We could, but I don't think my office floor is quite as comfortable as my bed."

"Definitely not," she agrees.

I kiss the tip of her nose as she hangs lifelessly in my arms.

"You're so cute sometimes," she mocks me.

"Shhh, don't tell anyone. I have a reputation to uphold."

14

E verly

I DRAG myself up the stairs of my apartment building close to ten p.m. It was another long, amazing week spent in Alec's bed. For the first time in years, I'm happy. Genuinely, down-to-my-bones happy. I forgot what this feeling was like. I only truly had it one other time in my life. And after years of pursuing it, then running from it, then longing for it, I've finally found it again. In the most unexpected place with the most unexpected person. I finally feel like I'm moving forward and not just running on a hamster wheel.

He didn't want me to leave. The memory makes me smile like a lovestruck fool. He begged me to stay, to spend one more night with him. And I wanted to, badly, but I had no clothes for work. And I'd never make it in on time if I had to stop at my apartment first. Our relationship is still so new, and there is that pesky rule of no fraternization. I'm walking a fine line being with Alec, as it is. I don't want to go totally off the deep end so soon. I understand why Lara risks it, though. I now finally understand what being with Luke means to her.

Being with Alec is quickly becoming something just as precious to me.

There's such a stupid tingle in my tummy. I'm falling in love. It's happening fast and furiously and with reckless abandon. And all I'm certain of at this very moment is that what I want above all else is a life worth living.

I turn the corner in the stairwell once I reach my floor, and when I see Tage leaning against my front door, all the happy fluttering in my stomach turns to sinking stones.

Fucker. This is the very last thing I need.

I haven't heard a peep from Tage since he invited himself to lunch. I could have stabbed him in the ear with a knife for the way he was acting. I don't know what gets into him sometimes. He's been an enigma since the moment I met him. He's impossible to read, moody, standoffish, and totally secretive. The only time he was ever open with me was when I was locked away in my tower like fucking Rapunzel. That was the only time he ever felt real. The circumstances were royally fucked up, but nothing in my life had ever felt more palpable. More tangible. I trusted him with everything I had, and he turned on me the first chance he got. I hated him for years. I still sort of hate him. As much as I wish he would just disappear for good, he made it crystal clear that would never happen. Not while there was still breath left in his lungs. *His words.* What I don't get is why? I'm stable, living on my own, have a job, an apartment, and an income. He did help with a few of those things, but I'm driving solely on my own now, so what the fuck gives?

Cut the damn cord already and let me live my fucking life. Maybe he's the reason I've had such a hard time moving forward because he is the anchor to my past. He's the part I didn't want to let go of. He hindered me from discovering who I am, from flourishing into adulthood because the child inside me ached for him.

He broke my fucking heart, and in the same instance my fucking soul.

But I've been piecing it back together, little by little, year after year, and I finally feel like somewhat of a whole woman. Yes, a woman. No longer a girl. No longer a child. A woman who is standing her ground and making her mark. A woman who is no longer going to ache for a man who doesn't want her. Who made his choice.

The time has finally come for me to make mine.

"Houdini makes yet another appearance." I agitatedly pull my keys out to open the door.

Tage stands next to me silently, his head down, body language tense, blond, wavy hair long and wild. I insert the key and just as the lock clicks, he shoots his arm out to stop me from entering my apartment.

I stop short, irritated as hell. "What is your problem?"

"Are you in love with him?" he asks straightforwardly.

Seriously?

"What if I am? What does it matter to you?" I bite. "It's none of your fucking business."

"*You* are my fucking business." He looks up, his hair falling into his hard eyes.

"I'm not a child anymore, Tage. Just let me go. Give me peace," my voice softens. I want to be free.

"I can't."

"Why? I'm fine. I don't need you to watch over me anymore."

"Because you have Alec?" he snarks.

I roll my eyes. "No, because I have learned to stand on my own two feet."

"I know you have."

"Then what the fuck is the problem?"

"I can't let go of you that easily."

"You let go of me years ago," I seethe.

"I never let go. I just did what was right. When it comes to you, I have always tried to do what was right."

"Well, you didn't. You made promises you didn't keep, you pushed me away, and you broke my fucking heart. And now you're here trying to take my happiness, too."

"I would never take your happiness," he protests. "The only thing I have ever wanted is for you to be happy."

"Then go away." Tears burn my eyes.

"I can't." His tone is rough.

"Why?" I demand.

Tage pulls out a folded piece of paper from the back of his jeans pocket and hands it to me.

I take it warily and unfold it. I nearly choke as I look at what's scribbled on the page.

"Why are you doing this? Why now? After all this fucking time." Tears stream out like a faucet from my eyes.

"I've wanted to tell you. I just didn't know how."

I break down right in the hallway, clutching the paper to my chest. The memories are unbearable. I wrote this note as a teenager. As a dependent child in love with a man she didn't even know. A heart and an arrow with "you" under the arrow, "me" over the heart. "4ever". I believed those words. I believed we'd be together forever. I was naïve. Clueless.

"Don't do this. Not now." I punch the paper into his chest. "Not when—"

My sentence is long gone under his abrupt kiss. He steals my words and breath the exact same way he did all those years ago. I fight at first, but we both know it's no use. The feelings are there, flooding over us like a tidal wave. I cry through the soul-crushing kiss as I wrap my arms around his neck and hold on for dear life. Tage crushes me against the door, his tongue reacquainting itself with my mouth. He kisses exactly the same. Dominantly, passionately, recklessly. My emotions split right in two as I succumb.

I have ached for him to touch me this way. I have ached to hear the sound of his voice in the dark of night, feel the warmth of his skin, experience the press of his lips. Ached for him to engulf my mind and my senses, like he once had. Ached to become lost in him, and him to become lost in me. I've ached to not be alone, if only for a painful moment. Because moments were all I had. All I was capable of. All I could bear.

Until now.

Reason is completely stripped away as Tage pushes us into my apartment. We barely make it inside before Tage is propping me up against the wall. I wrap my legs around his waist and attack his mouth as forcefully as he's attacking mine, our hips grinding, and our breathing ragged.

Is this really happening? A subconscious thought flits through my manic haze.

I feel the rigid length of his cock press right up against my clit and I confirm that it is. This is really happening, and I want it to. I want it to happen so bad I may spontaneously combust.

I don't even remember making it into the bedroom. I just remember falling back onto the mattress. I remember Tage ripping off his clothes and then mine.

Then there's just us, naked, desperate, and years of lost time from the past crashing over us.

There's no foreplay. No warm up, no nothing. Just Tage thrusting inside me. I scream, I see stars, I claw at his back as we fuck. It's passion elevated to another Earthly plane. It's pent-up aggression punching through the surface and shattering the glass ceiling.

I cry even more while he's inside me. It's painful and cathartic all at the same time. My body responds exactly how it did all those years ago. It aches, and throbs, and quivers. The walls of my pussy clamping down onto his cock for dear life.

"Don't disappear," I plead incoherently. "Please don't disappear."

"I'm not going anywhere," he promises. "You're mine. I'm yours," he heaves. "It's always been that way."

"Oh, God." My limbs lock up, a climax is coming, and it's going to be soul-shattering. "Tage," I expel. "Tage, please." He continues to punch his hips. I continue to claw at his back.

I can barely stand the buildup. I'm totally terrified of it.

Then it happens. He buries himself so deep I lose myself. I lose all concept of time and space and reality.

I come so hard I literally feel the rush of moisture saturate my inner thighs.

It's one big giant mess, my climax, my emotions, my life.

Tage comes violently, his orgasm matching the intensity of mine. He roars through the moment, and I know every single thing he's feeling.

A dynasty has fallen. Crashed. Burned. Disintegrated. And it's our turn to rebuild in the aftermath.

15

T age

I'M an asshole and I know it.

I, also, don't fucking care.

The only thing that matters at all is that Everly is back in her rightful place—in my arms. Naked, sated, and secure against my heated body.

She's sleeping soundlessly, her head resting upon my bare chest.

I run my fingers through her tangled hair, planning my thought process so I'm prepared when she wakes.

I went about it all wrong. The whole damn thing. The time. The place. The way. I ambushed her, but I felt backed into a corner. For eight damn years, I drowned in the taste of her innocence. I dreamt about what it felt like to lay beside her. She was my glimmer in the darkness, and I wanted it all back. Her taste, her touch, her virtue, her devotion.

She was slipping through my fingers, so I acted. There was no way in hell I was going to lose her again. Not a chance I was going to give her up again.

I thought I was doing the right thing all those years ago. I thought setting her free would liberate us both, but all it did was bind us together in an unbearable way.

I never wanted to condemn Everly by allowing her to love me. My situation is complicated. My life is nomadic. My career is dangerous. And my heart is split between love and risk.

But this, right here, right now, I can't give up. I tighten my arm around her.

There's a saying I once came across about the sun loving the moon so much he died every night just so she could breathe. That's the only way I can compare the last eight years, I died every day so Everly could live. The only problem was she didn't live. She died of heartbreak every fucking day, and it was all because of me. It was all my fault. I was a fool, but not anymore.

I wanted better for Everly. I wanted more. More than what I thought I could offer her, but now I see, no one can offer her more because all she's ever wanted was me. *My* love. So I plan to give it to her. Hand it over in spades so every day she can live and every night she can breathe.

16

E verly

I AM OFFICIALLY FUCKED UP.

I open my eyes to sunlight and the profile of a sleeping man. As I look at Tage, the events of the last night creep in like a living nightmare.

I should feel happy. I should be ecstatic that the man I have ached for the last eight years has let me back in, but I'm not. I'm a fucking mess, because my heart is filled with love for someone else just as much as it is filled with love for Tage.

The biggest problem with loving Tage is that it comes with strings attached. It comes with no guarantee. He has drifted in and out of my life for so long it's hard to decipher if he's even real. Hard to believe if his intentions are sincere. Truth be told, I don't know the man I went to bed with last night. I only know the memory of who he was when we were together. That's who I cling to. He looks the same, he speaks the same, he makes love the same, but is he the same? Is that person I fell madly in love with years ago still inside? Is he sleeping next to me now? There's too many questions to ponder before coffee. Before I'm even fully awake.

And on top of it all, there's Alec.

The guilt begins to eat me alive. I care about him. *A lot.* I know what heartbreak feels like, and I would never wish it on another human being, especially one, dare I say, I might love. Maybe I was better off alone? Maybe the universe was trying to tell me something. Solitude is safe.

I glance at the clock. It's nearly six-thirty. I can't stay here, but I dread going to work. I can't look Alec in the eyes. Not yet.

Maybe I should just run away?

A ridiculous solution, but appealing, nonetheless.

I try to slide out of bed as stealthy as possible, but Tage's arm shoots out and snatches my wrist before I make it six centimeters.

"Where do you think you're going?" He smiles with his eyes closed.

"It's Friday. Work."

His eyebrows crease, but his lids remain shut. "Blow it off. Spend the day in bed with me. We have a lot to catch up on."

For some reason, that request infuriates me. He expects me to just drop everything just because he's graced my sheets with his presence.

"I can't. That's not how adulting works." I yank my wrist from his grasp.

"I'm sensing some hostility." Tage pops his eyes open, and the brown ringing his pupils illuminates in the sun.

"What the fuck gave it away?"

"You're mad? Why?"

Why? *Why?* We just created a monumental mess of my life. Am I supposed to be happy?

"Ugh." I toss the covers off and escape into the bathroom, locking the door behind me to gain some space. My apartment isn't all that big, but I'm grateful for the multiple rooms.

I wash my face, do my business, and skip the shower. I just need to go.

"Everly." Tage voices my name while sitting up in my bed. How many times have I dreamed of this exact moment? This exact situation. Countless, for years and years, and when I finally give up the fantasy, it becomes a nightmarish reality.

The worst-possible timed encounter in my entire life.

I grab some work clothes from the closet and throw them on. Tie my hair back in a ponytail in record time, and don't even bother with makeup. If anyone asks, I had a restless night's sleep. It's not so far from the truth. "We need to talk."

"No, we don't," I shut him down. "I just need to go."

"Don't go," he pushes.

"I have to. I can't do this. Not right now." I start to make my escape, but Tage is up and blocking the door faster than I can blink. I try not to notice that he is still gloriously naked, tattooed, and toned. I look away. Temptation is the last thing I need.

"Why can't you do this now?"

My heart wilts. "It's too hard."

"Why?" He steps closer and touches my face. My eyes become watery. *Please don't.*

"How can we go through this again? You broke my heart." All the years of suppressed pain shoot to the surface. "I trusted you. I loved you. I needed you." Tears fall.

"I was here."

"No, you weren't." I look up into his hazel eyes. "Not the way you promised you'd be."

"I thought I was doing the right thing—"

"Well, you didn't." I push past him.

"Ever," Tage calls after me, but he doesn't follow me into the living room.

Just as I make it to the front door, I notice the crumpled-up pink paper on the floor. I scoop it up, stick it in my pocket, and leave.

My emotions fracturing from the pain of the past, the felicity of the present, and uncertainty of the future.

lec

I'VE TEXTED EVERLY TWICE this morning with no reply.

I had to go straight to the courthouse, so I wasn't able to catch her in the office, which totally sucks since I've grown accustomed to her greeting me straight out of the elevators every morning.

I hurry down the stone courthouse stairs and to one of the firm's Town Cars waiting on Worth Street. I hop into the back seat and find a surprise. The woman who had stopped me on the street a few days ago is perched comfortably behind the front seat.

"Hello again, Mr. Prescott."

"What the fuck —"

"Everyone has a price. The driver is taking a walk," she smirks darkly. "So we could have some privacy."

I leer. *That driver is so fired.*

"You have three seconds to get out of this car."

"Or what? You're going to scream? Yell fire?" She pokes fun at me.

"I'm not sure you know who I am —"

"Oh, I know exactly who you are, Mr. Prescott. A poor boy from upstate New York who worked his ass off to pay for an Ivy League education and land a high-profile job in New York. It's like a fairytale. The pauper has become the prince. Your parents must be so proud."

"They are." I snarl. "Now what the fuck do you want?"

"You, Mr. Prescott. You have come to be extremely valuable to me."

"Valuable how?"

"You are very close to someone. Someone I need to get close to."

"Everly." I already know the answer.

"Yes."

"Why?"

"Not your concern. But I need you to deliver her."

"Deliver her? She's not a goddamn package."

"She's important to both of us."

"I highly doubt that. I won't do a goddamn thing until you tell me what you want from her."

"That's between me and her."

"Well, then, you're going to have to find another way to contact her. Get out—"

"Mr. Prescott, you care for Everly, do you not?"

I pause, biting my tongue. *Of course, I love her.* "We have a working relationship."

The woman scoffs. "Is that what you're calling it? To save face? Or your job?"

I remain silent.

"Mr. Prescott, this can be as easy or as hard as you make it. Deliver Everly to me, when and where I text you."

"Never gonna happen."

"Fine." She shrugs aloofly. "It'll be a pity when your firm finds out you were having an affair with a secretary." Her tone is mild yet threatening.

"Are you trying to blackmail me?" I snort. "Go ahead. Tell them. Let the whole world know. I don't give a fuck."

Her brown stare sharpens. "Okay, then, how do you think they'll feel when they find out you've been taking kickbacks from clients, and tampering with evidence, *and* having an affair with a fellow employee?"

My blood pressure skyrockets. "Those first two things aren't true."

"Your firm doesn't know that. I have some very powerful people in my pocket, Mr. Prescott. You're not the only one with connections. I can make things very difficult. I can take away your career. Your fairytale. I can ruin your life."

"You're bluffing."

"Am I?" She pulls on the handle and the door pops open. "I don't want this to get ugly or violent, Mr. Prescott. But I'm willing to do what I must to get what I want. And Everly has something I want."

"Which is?"

Her red lips curl up, but she doesn't satisfy me with an answer. "I'll be in touch. Keep your phone close."

She slips out of the car and then out of fucking sight.

I'm blinded by red as my emotions go haywire.

I gave Everly the benefit of the doubt, but now it's time to confront her.

I RUSH out of the elevator to find Everly in her usual spot behind her desk. I texted her two more times on the way over to the office, and again there was no reply. After my little rendezvous with the woman in the car, I am positive something is up, and I'm going to find out what it is. Right-fucking-now.

"Miss Paige, can I see you in my office, please?" I rush by the front desk with urgency and yank open the double-glass doors. I hold them ajar waiting for her, but she doesn't follow.

We stare at each other, a storm-bed of tension bubbling beneath just the two of us.

I wait only a moment more before blowing through the doorway. In my office, I expel a volatile breath. Something is wrong. So, so wrong, and somehow, I landed myself right in the middle of all the shit.

There's a soft knock at the door, and I look up to find Everly standing there meekly. She's a hot mess in high heels. Her clothes are wrinkled. She has no makeup on, there are bags under her eyes, her skin is pale, her hair is frizzy, and her glasses are sitting crooked on her nose. But worst of all, her body language is standoffish. Her arms are wrapped around her waist, and her head is hung low.

Something twists painfully in my stomach, and I'm uneasy on my feet. The fear of the unknown combined with an untrusting duress has me teetering on a razor-sharp edge.

"You wanted to see me?" Her sentence is cold and distant. I know we're at work and need to keep up appearances, but right now, the distance feels too damn real.

"Shut the door." I jerk my chin.

"I don't think that's a good idea."

She won't take one step farther into my office.

"We need to talk. *Privately*," I insist.

Her eyes widen, almost fearfully.

"I can't do this right now, Alec. Not here," her voice strains.

"Do what? Talk? I know—"

"Alec," Mr. Turner, the firm's founding partner, picks the most inopportune time to interrupt us. He breezes past Everly with a file folder in his hand, heavily engrossed in its contents. "The clients are here for the deposition, but I have some questions about these notes you jotted down. Let's talk before we get started."

I inwardly heave. This day just keeps getting better and better.

"I'll be in your office in just a minute."

"Nonsense, we're here now. No need to shuffle rooms." The older man with graying hair and intimidating power suit drops the folder onto my desk, and it sounds like rocks hitting pavement. *Worst. Timing. Ever.*

Everly clears her throat. "I'll let you two talk." She steps backward away from us. Mr. Turner looks at her over his shoulder, as if just realizing she was standing there.

"Are you feeling all right, Miss Paige? You don't look well." He sounds genuinely concerned.

"No, Mr. Turner," her voice squeaks. "I'm not feeling that well."

"Go home then, young lady. Get yourself well. Can't have one of our rising stars all run down." He winks at her.

"I'll do that." Everly smiles weakly, glancing at me. Our swift eye contact feels like a puncture wound. Something is so fucking wrong. I can feel it in my bones.

I'm locked in a steel box. Trapped. I can't demand her to stay, and I can't avoid the man standing in front of me. Too much is at stake. Too many careers on the line. Too many emotions blowing in the wind.

Everly disappears, and my heart crumples like a piece of paper. A wicked fear grabbing hold.

In the short time we've been together, she has come to mean so much more to me than I could have ever imagined. Her absence has me longing for her, and she's only been gone several seconds. Without her by my side, a piece of me is missing. I handed over part of myself, and I didn't even realize it. And she took it with no hesitation.

The question now is what is going to happen to that piece of me?

What is going on with Everly, and how can I protect her from whatever it is?

18

T age

I WANDER THE CITY AIMLESSLY. Thoughts of Everly consuming my mind. Last night. Every heavenly second of it I relive over and over. And every hellish moment of this morning, as well. A tumultuous uncertainty is storming inside me. She regrets it. She regrets being with me because another man has moved into her heart. A heart that is supposed to belong solely to me. A heart that has always been mine. Even when I destroyed it. The wrong thing for the right reasons has never sucked so much.

There is no other option for us now, though. I won't let her go again, so whatever she's feeling for Alec Prescott is going to evaporate. I'm going to make her forget him. I'm going to make it like he never existed.

Everly belongs to me, and no one is going to come between us again.

No one is going to fuck it up again. Especially me.

I sit on a park bench with the warm June air rippling the waves of my overgrown hair. I'm on my fifth cup of coffee and jittery as hell. It has nothing to do with the caffeine, though. I just want to be with Everly. I want to be standing beside her, inhaling her sweet scent and running my hands along her curves. I want her smiling at me the way she once did. Kissing me passionately, sighing contently. Her sounds always get me. Make me crumble. Make me hard, make me wanton, make me happy.

She is the only thing that has ever made me truly happy.

My phone vibrates in my pocket, and I check the message. Work. Always work. It's my addiction and my downfall. I can never say no because I live for the high. For the danger. For the unknown.

The message from the private caller reads:

A FRIENDLY FACE *has made an appearance in* New York. *Thought you should know just in case you wanted to say hi.*

I SCROLL though the several surveillance pictures that accompany the text, and the spike in my blood pressure almost makes my head explode.

I jump up off the bench, sending my coffee flying as I rush to the closest street. I hail a cab in record time as I track Everly down. She doesn't know it, but I'm tapped into the GPS on her phone so I know where she is at all times.

A quick ride through midtown and I am jumping out the taxi door right in front of her apartment building. I refrained from stalking her all day, for sanity's sake, but it's after five, so it's no surprise she's home.

I race up the three flights of stairs and almost barrel through her front door, but I stop myself at the last second. We are navigating on delicate waters right now, and the last thing I want to do is upset her more. We have a lot to talk about. A lot, way more than just what transpired last night.

"Ever!" I bang on the door impatiently. "Ever, it's me. We need to talk." I continue to pound. I won't stop until she answers. Moments later, the hinges squeak as the door swings open.

"Tage, this isn't a good time." Her words vaporize as I look beyond where she's standing and see Alec sitting on the couch.

My protective instincts kick into overdrive. Shoving Everly out of the way, I go after Alec like a raging bull. Pulling a Glock from the back holster of my waistband, I pounce on top of him, shoving the barrel of the gun into his mouth.

"Tell me who the fuck you are," I snarl as I squeeze the trigger and his cheeks. "What the fuck do you want with Everly, and how do you know Vicki?"

Alec just shakes his head, muffled sounds spilling out of his mouth as Everly screams at me. It's all a bit chaotic in the room, but the force is necessary.

Anger, rage, vigilance, and possessiveness flare inside me as I push the barrel farther down this motherfucker's throat. He gags, and I find immense satisfaction from the reaction.

"TAGE!" Everly's shrill voice cuts through my hysteria. *"Get the fuck off him!"* She pulls at my arm. *"Please!"* Her earnest tone reins me in.

With ragged breaths, I withdraw the gun, but I don't move off Alec. I want answers, and I want them right fucking now.

He pants, catching his breath, then a shitstorm rages in his eyes. "Asshole." He shoots off the couch, sending us both to the floor. We grapple, a punch thrown here and there. He lands a good one on my cheek. I retaliate by splitting his lip wide open.

"*Stop!*" Everly shrieks, and then the gun goes off. I'm on my feet in a split second, corralling her against the wall.

"Are you fucking crazy?" I slip the gun out of her hand before she kills someone.

"No, I'm fucking pissed," she snaps.

"Not an excuse to fire a weapon."

"You were about to blow my boyfriend's fucking head off." I wince at the word boyfriend.

"Only out of necessity." I re-holster the gun and glance back at Alec to make sure he isn't getting any funny ideas. We don't need any more vigilante moves.

Pulling my cell phone out of my back pocket, I hit one button to dial the private number that so generously sent me the surveillance pics.

"Tage?"

"Simon. I need you to run some interference. Use my GPS location. Intercept any responses to shots fired at this location." I glare into Everly's eyes. "It was an accidental discharge."

"Done." I hear Simon typing away faster than lightning on the other end.

"Stay out of trouble and keep your gun in your pants." *Click.*

"Who the fuck is Simon? Why do you have a gun? Actually, why don't you just start with who the fuck you are," Alec erupts.

"I should be the one interrogating you," I bark.

"Stop!" Everly explodes. "Just stop. Both of you. We all just need to get on the same page."

"Well, I would love to know what fucking page that is." Alec agitatedly wipes some blood from his lip. His tan, pretty-boy suit is all messed up and splattered with red stains. My ego inflates from his disheveled appearance. *Take that, pretty boy.*

"Maybe if we can talk like civilized adults and not act like hormonal teenagers" — she is clearly directing that statement at me — "we can avoid any more bloodshed."

"Where's the fun in that?" I almost want to pout.

Ever rolls her eyes. I really am just an adolescent teen in a man's body, and I'm secure enough to admit it. My impulsiveness is part of the reason I'm still alive.

My motto? Always be one step ahead — and have bigger gonads than Godzilla.

"You can't come barging into my life whenever the fuck you feel like it, Tage," Everly downright scolds me. "I have a life, and a person I care about. You need to accept that." Something in her statement sounds so final. *Is she choosing him over me?*

Gritting my teeth, I focus on the issue at hand. I didn't barge into her apartment because she was with another man, although after last night, I sure as fuck would. I'm not letting her go so easily.

"You can't trust him," I announce loudly enough so the whole room can hear.

"Like hell," Alec growls, taking a step toward me.

"Explain." Everly jumps between us with her arms out. She was always a spirited one.

Sighing, I press a few buttons on my phone and show her the evidence. These images could potentially crush her. Hurting her is the last thing I want, but I'll be here to pick up all her broken pieces. She won't deal with this alone. She won't be alone, ever again. I hold up the screen and show her the pictures. Several of an older woman and a man conversing on the street and getting in and out of the same car.

"Is that—" She squints. She isn't wearing her glasses.

"Alec, yes," I bite.

"No." She grabs the phone from me. "My . . . *mom?*"

"Your mom?" Alec spies over her shoulder to get a look of his own.

"It is," I confirm. Everly stares at the picture heavily for several long seconds.

"She looks so different." She frowns.

"You mean she looks clean?"

Everly nods sadly.

"Looks can be deceiving," I warn her.

"This is the woman you were telling me about?" Everly glances back at Alec.

"What?" I stiffen.

"That's her," Alec confirms.

"What am I missing here?" I ask them both.

"Well" — Everly hands me back my phone — "before you busted in here like Rambo, Alec was telling me that he was approached by a woman who was threatening me. And him."

"She threatened her?" I snarl.

"She said Everly has something she wants. She tried to blackmail me, but it didn't work, so she resorted to threats. I'm concerned for Everly's safety. She didn't look well at work. I knew something was up. I confronted her."

Definitely not the explanation I was expecting. Or hoping for. The ideal situation would be Alec was working with Everly's mother, which would give me the perfect excuse to kill him. But no such luck.

"What is she after?" I press.

"No idea. She wouldn't tell me. She just wanted me to deliver Everly when and where she texted."

"Well, that shit isn't going to happen," I grunt.

"I think I might know what she wants." Everly wrings her hands together, pacing her apartment.

"Which is?" Both Alec and I are completely enthralled.

"A key, maybe?"

"A key to what?" I ask.

"I don't know." Her green eyes jump frantically between me and Alec. She's hesitant to talk, and it's for a host of reasons. "I have to tell him," Everly beseeches me.

"Ever—" I shake my head sternly.

"Tell me what?"

Everly and I just stare each other down. She's chewing the shit out of her lip, fraying at the seams. The past is burying us faster than an avalanche, and she is the only one who can make the decision to let the truth save us or destroy us.

"If we tell him, he becomes a part of it. No turning back," I warn her.

"He's already a part of it." She makes a good point.

Dejection reflects in her eyes as she continually glances between me and Alec. She's deliberating. She cares about him. I can see it, and it kills me.

"We have to." Her voice strains.

"Tell me what?" Alec demands. He's in the dark, and he doesn't like it one bit.

I can't blame him. It's a shitty place to be. Unfortunately, sometimes, the dark is the safest option.

"My name isn't Everly Paige." Everly shuffles towards Alec. "Well, my birth name anyway." Alec stands still as a statue as Everly speaks. As do I. "My real name is Destiny Star Reynolds. My mom was, *is,* a drug addict, and she got wrapped up with some really bad people when I was young. She had married this guy who was a huge drug dealer in Chicago. He sort of became obsessed with me when I turned thirteen. He locked me away in my room and kept me like a prisoner." She clears her throat. That time was so hard for her. The isolation, the loneliness. I can remember it like it was yesterday. Picturing her standing in that window, a sad image of a girl longing for something, for someone, to save her. For some reason, the idea popped into my head that that someone could be me. Climbing into her window was the best choice and the biggest mistake of my life.

"Did —" Alec clears his throat uncomfortably. "Did he hurt you?"

I know what he's getting at. I thought the same thing at first. Why else do you keep a young girl locked up from the world?

"No. Never. He never touched me. It wasn't like that. I was more like a doll. It was weird, no doubt, but he never abused me."

Alec visibly sighs. Yes, it is a comfort knowing he never hurt her. I would have killed Gunner right there on the spot if he had. It would have fucked my whole career up, but it would have been totally worth it.

"So, how exactly do you two know each other?" Alec points between the two of us. Ah, the burning question.

"I took her virginity." I slide my arm around Ever.

"*Tage.*"

Alec scowls, and my life is complete.

Everly pushes me off her. "Our past is complicated."

"It's going to become less complicated because we are getting back together." I slip my arm protectively around Everly once again.

"What?" Alec visually slices Everly open with a look shaper than a straight blade. Scary.

"Um, no, we are not." And she pushes me away once again.

"Then what was last night about?"

"Last night?" Alec repeats, his facial expression hardening.

"Tage," Everly growls at me. It's adorable.

"Yeah, we had sex." I look pointedly at Alec. "It was incredible." I twist the knife even deeper. *Asshole. I know.*

"Tage," Everly explodes.

Okay, maybe I'm being a little too loose-lipped. It's really not nice to kiss and tell.

The look on Alec's face is priceless, though. I wish I could take a picture. He is trying so hard to keep it together, but the angry shade of red his skin is turning completely gives him away. *Need a better poker face, buddy.*

I shouldn't be enjoying this so much, but I am. *You're going to be out of Everly's life in three-point-two seconds, and I'll make sure she never thinks about you again.*

"Alec, I'm so sorry. I wanted to tell you. It was an accident. A mistake."

Mistake?

"I don't know how you accidentally fall into bed with someone, Everly."

Ooooh, his tone is ice cold. It even makes me shiver.

"Alec, please. I'm sorry. Can we just talk about this? About everything?" Everly is nearly on her knees begging this jerkoff to hear her out. To forgive her.

"Ever." I tug on her arm. "Let him go. You don't need him." *You have me.*

Everly lashes out at me, shoving me away. "Yes, I do. I do need him. You don't get to decide for me, Tage. You don't get to just waltz right back into my life and expect me to drop everyone that I love. Last night was a mistake. It should have never happened." The words are painful. Painful for me to hear and painful for her to say, because I know they're not entirely true. I know Everly Paige better than anyone, and last night meant as much to her as it did to me, but Alec has staked a claim on a bigger piece of her heart than I anticipated.

"I think I need some air." Alec brushes by us with a ghostly expression on his face. The dude is clearly fucked up, and not in the good way.

"Alec, please don't go. Please, let's talk about this." She catches his hand at the last second, but he instantly pulls away. She's crushed.

She'll get over it. Over him. Eventually.

Alec slams the door behind him, and all that's left is us. Exactly the way it should be. The way it should have always been.

"Hey." I take her arms and turn her to face me. There are heavy tears running down her cheeks. "It'll be okay. I'm here."

She peers up at me with a dark expression. It's quite frankly a little disturbing.

Then, silently as a sniper, she slaps me right across the face.

lec

O<small>UTSIDE ON THE STREET</small>, I suck on my vape pen like it's a damn oxygen stick.

My mind is fucking reeling. This day, I have no words to describe it. I woke up on top of the world, and right now I'm buried beneath it.

Everything is bruised — my heart, my lip, my ego.

The first time in forever I take a chance on someone, and it blows up in my face.

"Rough day, huh?" Tage suddenly nudges me. I glance over at him to find a surprise. A fading red hand print graffitied across his cheek.

"You could say that." I begin to walk away. The last person I want to be around is *him*.

To my utter dismay, he follows.

"Get lost," I spit.

"We should talk."

"I think you've done enough talking."

"Not even a little bit." He latches onto my bicep and directs me into a dark pub on the street corner. "Drinks will help."

"Nothing will fucking help." I inhale one more puff of my vape.

"Alcohol always helps. It's the cure-all. Especially when you drink so much of it you forget you even exist."

"I wouldn't mind forgetting you exist."

Tage just grunts, but he doesn't seem bothered by my snarky comment at all.

The bar is a dump. Dusty, ancient furnishings and a bartender older than the day.

"Two shot glasses and a bottle of Jack." Tage slaps the bar top.

"No Jack, sonny, this is an Irish bar. You want whiskey, it's Jameson or bust," the bartender croaks.

"We'll have Jameson, then."

Definitely not my first choice.

It takes the elderly man what feels like a year to get off his stool, grab the green bottle and two shot glasses, and place them in front of us. By the time he does, I'm thirstier than the fucking desert. At least Tage has the good sense to pour my shot first. It goes down like fire, but I surprisingly like the burn. I grab the bottle neck and pour another one, and then one more.

"Do you want to race? Because I can totally keep up." He slams his second shot.

"I just want to forget."

"Forget what?"

"This day ever fucking happened."

"Yeah, shitty days suck."

"Why are you here?"

"The alcohol?" He shakes his shot glass like *duh*.

I'm not amused. I'm pissed, I'm miserable, and I want to punch him right in the fucking face. *Again.* "And to talk."

"Right. Talk." I pound another shot.

"You throw a pretty good right hook for a pretty boy."

"I wasn't always a pretty boy. I just dress the part perfectly."

"I wasn't always a shithead, but I dress the part perfectly, too." Down Tage's hatch goes another shot.

"Can we get this *talk* over with, please?" I just want to go home and smoke myself stupid.

"Don't blame Ever for what happened. I initiated it. I took advantage of our situation."

"And what situation is that?" I question.

"She loves me."

I nearly puke in my mouth. "Are you just here to twist the knife a little deeper? Do you get off on crushing people's emotions? I'll admit, I can act like an asshole sometimes, but you are straight up ruthless."

"I'll answer those questions in order. No, I'm not here to twist the knife deeper, and yes, I do find some minor enjoyment in crushing other people's emotions. It's probably just because I'm a miserable bastard myself. See what I did there? A little psychoanalysis on myself."

He sounds so delighted. "Freud would be proud." *More brown liquid in the glass, please.*

"Look, mine and Everly's past is complicated. It's tangled, and painful, and utterly complex. I hurt her deeply when I thought I was trying to protect her. I thought I was doing the right thing. And for a long time I believed that, but lately, not so much." Tage talks to the shot glass he is spinning in his fingers.

"Am I supposed to feel sorry for you?"

"No. I'm just trying to make you understand where Everly is coming from. Where we're both coming from."

"Can you explain how you 'hurt her deeply'?" I regurgitate his words.

"Yes, but I'll need another shot first." He grabs the bottle. Tage pours one shot and then follows right behind it with another.

"Ahhh, okay." He seemingly gears up for this explanation.

"Everly was sixteen when I met her. I was twenty-four. It was my first undercover assignment."

"You're a cop?"

"Mmm." He winces, "Not exactly. I work for a private contractor called Endeavor. We sort of work on the fringe of the law. We're the ones who break the rules and don't exactly get in trouble. It's very involved, and yet what we do is extremely important."

"So, you were there to take Everly's stepfather down?"

"Not exactly. Gunner was moving up the ranks pretty damn fast, and we were enlisted to collect intel. Find the bigger fish, so to speak. You don't grow that fast or that quickly without knowing some pretty powerful people or making some pretty significant contacts. We needed to find out who was funding him. Where he was getting his influx of drugs. And I did. I also fell in love with Ever. It was a massive no-no. Getting emotionally and physically involved with a minor while working undercover. I was there to do a job, not get off. But I found myself doing both. The girl in the window intrigued me. I tied to ignore her, but every night I saw her staring out into that courtyard, and I just had to find out who she was. Why she was there. And so much more ended up happening."

I can actually see the regret sketched on his face.

"So, how did you hurt her?"

"I made promises."

"What kind of promises?"

"I promised I would take care of her. That I would always be there for her. And I kept those promises, just not in the way she expected."

"So, you were fucking her, whispering sweet nothings in her ear, and then you pulled the rug out from under her? Am I following correctly?"

"That law school degree didn't go to waste." He clicks his tongue and points at me. "I wasn't just fucking her. I genuinely loved her. I *still* genuinely love her. My cover was blown somehow. Gunner found out about me, so I had to act fast. The night everything went down, the night his compound was raided, I promised Everly I would take care of her. I wasn't even supposed to be there, but I couldn't not warn her. She hadn't seen the outside world in three years. The only people she had contact with were me and Gunner, and her mother when the fancy striked. I *did* take care of Ever. I made sure she got a fresh start. But I couldn't be part of that new life. Not the way she wanted me to. She wanted us to be together. To be a family, but my work, my life, it was just too complicated. I didn't want that for her. I wanted her to be happy. I wanted her to be free. I wanted so much more for her than just . . . *me.*"

"So you walked away?"

"In a sense, yes. I would pop in to check on her now and again. I always kept tabs, but she hated me. Resented me. I broke her fucking heart, and I knew it, but I couldn't stay away. Deep down those feelings were always still stirring. And then she met you." His wavy, blond hair is shielding his eye and cheek of his profile, but I don't have to see his expression to know. Seeing her with me drove him batshit crazy. The same kind of crazy it drove me when I found out they were together last night. Knife. Stab. Wound. Chest.

"What a fucking pair we are." I down another shot, my throat nearly numb from the burn of the whiskey.

"What a fucking pair," Tage agrees as he follows my lead.

"So, what the fuck are you two sad sacks gonna do about it?" the elderly bartender croaks from his stool in the corner. Who knew he could hear so far?

Tage and I exchange an unsure look. We have rammed head first into an impasse.

"My brother and I felt for the same girl once," the old man muses.

"Oh, yeah, and what did you do about it?" Tage asks gruffly.

The old man shrugs. "What our mother taught us to do. Share."

Tage and I are silent as we absorb this response. *Share?*

We don't get to analyze the response for long as a middle-aged man storms into the bar.

"Pop. Jesus, Pop, we have been looking all over for you."

Tage and I just stare confused as the man strides across the cracked wood floor to where his elderly father is sitting.

"I'm right where I should be," the old man bristles.

"The bar is closed. We sold it. You can't keep coming back here."

Tage and I freeze. *Closed? Sold? Oh, shit.*

"I'm sorry." The man with a graying goatee and button-up shirt turns to us. "He has dementia. He's supposed to be in a nursing home, but he keeps sneaking out and coming back here. We sold the bar a few days ago." He looks at his father with pity. "It's been his home for over thirty years."

"It's still my home. It always will be, Justin."

"James, Dad. *James,*" the man corrects him.

"James." The old man inspects his son's face. They share the same features, prominent nose and small, inset eyes.

"I'm sorry. I'm going to have to ask you two to leave. No one should be here. Especially him." He frowns.

"We're leaving." Tage shoots his last shot. "Do you mind if we take the bottle, though?"

"No," the man smirks. "Consider it a thanks for keeping this one out of trouble."

"Anytime." Tage hops out of his chair, and I follow.

"Later, old-timer." Tage salutes him.

"Remember what I said, boys. Share," he responds almost parentally.

We exit the bar on that note.

Share?

"I think we should go check on Everly." Tage starts walking in the direction of her apartment building.

"Both of us?" I catch up to him.

"You heard the man. Share."

"Are you serious?" I pull his arm, stopping him short.

"Of course, I am. Haven't you ever shared a woman before?"

"Define the context. A drunken threesome in college, yes."

"You're not so prissy, huh?" Tage smiles.

"I'm not prissy at all. Nice suits don't equate to picture perfect. And this is Everly we're talking about. She isn't just some random hook-up."

"She isn't," he agrees. "Which is why I think this is a great idea."

"Explain," I huff.

"Listen, Everly has gotten the short end of the stick most of her life. With her parents, with me. She deserves all the love she can get. It's like the ideal romance novel. The bad boy and the businessman. What woman would refuse that?" Tage is smug.

"Um, a sane one," I contradict.

"Gotta live a little, man. Chase more than just ambulances." Tage starts walking again, cockier than a rooster in a hen house.

"I don't fucking chase ambulances, and I live plenty," I argue.

"Well, I'm not giving Everly up. So, either I go into her apartment alone, or you come with me."

"What if she doesn't want you? What if she chooses me?"

"Why even present her with the option?"

"So, you want to manipulate her into a threesome?"

"No. I want to offer her everything she deserves. Which is both of us. You have three blocks to think about it. I'm all in."

"You make heavy decisions pretty quick," I point out.

"Life is too short to mull over bullshit. I know what I want, and I go for it."

"This has the potential to get messy."

"If we're lucky." Tage pops his eyebrows and smiles salaciously.

"That's not what I meant." I elbow him, but the prospect is inviting.

I imagine the scenario the whole way to Everly's apartment building — two guys, one girl, lots and lots of orgasms. It isn't a torturous thought.

Once in front of her door, both Tage and I prepare for a beat.

Getting dirty doesn't bother me, but can I share the woman I love?

I'm sure as hell about to find out.

20

E verly

I HUG my pillow the same way I did as a child as the tears flow down my face. Not surprisingly, they dry faster than they did back then.

Barely anything has changed over the last eight years. I'm still alone. I'm still sad. I'm still isolated, except now, my emotions are hardened.

No matter how much I try to change my situation, it seems I'm cursed to repeat the past in one way or another.

I should be falling apart. I should be crumbling under the heartbreak, but I'm not. I've become way too good at saying goodbye. At dealing with heartache. Every time Tage walked out the door, it desensitized me a little more while killing me at the same time.

The pain was so severe I had to learn to smother it. The more I hurt, the less I would allow myself to cry. Until today.

The love I so desperately wanted just slipped through my fingers.

Tage ruined everything, and yet, like a desperate, love-struck teenager, I'm hoping he comes back.

Foolishly, I want them both to come back.

I'm in love with them both and have no idea what to do about it.

Choose?

Impossible.

Sacrifice them both?

I can't bring myself to imagine my life with one and not the other.

It almost doesn't make sense. They both offer me something completely unique. Two primary colors that saturate my world with pigment when mixed together.

An emotional kaleidoscope that conquers my full attention. My entire existence.

Impossible positions. That's what I'm constantly presented with, nothing but impossible positions.

For once in my goddamn life I just want things to be easy.

There's a light knock on my bedroom door.

"Go away," I grumble, not really meaning it at all.

"We both know that's not what you want." Tage enters with Alec right behind him. I pop my head up off the pillow confused, slightly elated, and completely terrified.

The two men swallow the small room, making it feel tinier than it already is.

Each one claims a side of the bed, and all I can do is sit perfectly still, watching their every move.

The energy in the air is off. It's thick with tension, and something else. Something I can't identify. I can feel it, though. Tugging at my core and wrapping around my gut.

My throat is dry, and my heartbeat is rapid.

Tage sits on the edge of the bed first.

Placing his hand over mine, he says, "I'm sorry, love."

My jaw drops. Tage never apologizes. For anything. He's always stood by his decisions without hesitation. It's one of the things I equally love and hate about him. "I'm sorry for everything. For today. For yesterday. For the last eight years." His hazel eyes are so raw. So genuine. They're the same eyes that used to look at me all those years ago. A lump forms in my throat. I don't want to cry, but I'm on the brink.

"I'm so mad at you," I whisper. I want to scream it, but I can't. My voice is nearly gone.

"I know. That's why I'm here. Why we're both here." He glances over at Alec.

I'm more confused than ever.

Alec touches the dimple in my forehead, the same way he did in the elevator that day. It's a familiar gesture that sets me at ease.

"Neither one of us wants to you give up. And we don't want to put you in a position to choose." Alec exhales a heavy breath. The tension in the room cracks like a piece of an iceberg just fell into the sea.

"I'm not sure I understand." My attention jumps between them.

"We know that you do." Tage picks up my hand and places a kiss on the inside of my wrist. He's being sweet. He's being sensitive. He's being very un-Tage like.

Alec then sits on the bed, and all my senses heighten to red alert. What's happening here?

Alec presses a soft kiss on my neck, and my silent question is answered.

Holy shit.

"Are you two fucking around right now?" I could almost explode.

"We would never. Not about this. Not with you," Tage declares resolutely as the emotional strain continuously applies pressure. I'm a joint ready to break.

Taking Alec's hand, I slip his arm around my waist for support. Him I trust. As much as I want Tage, the past eight years weighs heavily on me. It's my burden. I don't know if I can withstand another one of his heartbreaks.

Alec tightens his hold, and Tage clearly sees our connection. There's worry in his eyes. Those big, all-consuming, hazel eyes that I have dreamt about continuously for eight years. I missed them looking at me like that. Like I was as glorious as the entire galaxy.

"I don't know if I can do it. Let you in again." The words burn leaving my lips. I love this man, I always have, but my trust in him has diminished.

Tage nearly crushes my hand as he holds it with both of his. "Ever, I can't live without you. And I don't think you can live without either of us. Take a chance. One more, that's all I'm asking. One last chance for me to make it right."

I shake my head, unsure.

"You won't be left with nothing," Alec hums in my ear. It's like he can read my mind. He's uncovered my deepest fear and brought it to light. I turn my head to look back at him. "Promise me." I want promises. I want guarantees. "Nothing" isn't an option.

"I promise." He doesn't hesitate.

"I promise, too," Tage adds gruffly.

My brain splits in two. The notion feels so farfetched I can barely comprehend it.

"Both of you?" The question is more rhetorical than anything. I can have them both? No choosing? No sacrifice? No heartache?

"Both of us," Tage confirms.

"If that's what you want," Alec adds.

"And you're both okay with that?" The question sounds befuddled.

"We're here, aren't we?" Alec kisses my neck again, and my eyes involuntarily close. His lips are warm and consoling. They're everything I fucking need.

"All you have to do is say yes, and we're yours." Tage touches my cheek, and the contact feels like fire.

I hesitate, but not because I don't want them. Because my ability to speak has up and vanished.

I breathe heavily and swallow hard searching for the word. The one word that will bring us together and set us all free.

"Yes," I squeak. It's all I can force out. But it's enough. Enough for both of them. And enough for me.

I fall into an abyss then. Two men, two promises, two lifelines to my heart. Without thinking, I kiss Alec as I hold Tage's hand to my chest. I don't know the protocol. I don't know what's really happening. All I know is the iceberg is melting, crumbling into the cold sea, taking with it my reservations, my fears, my pain, and all my insecurities.

There's blind movement after that. A scurry of hands, a fluster of lips, and an array of urgent touches.

Before I know it, I'm on my knees sandwiched between two men who steal my breath.

Two mouths moving up and down my neck and over my bare shoulders once Alec removes my dress shirt.

The cool draft against my sensitive skin makes me alarmingly aware of what exactly is happening.

What I'm allowing to happen. The craziness of it all. But I want it. Want them. Both of them. For once in my life, I want to be selfish. I want to let go and forget about all the rights and indulge in all the wrongs. Even though this doesn't feel wrong. It's strange. It's new. But not wrong. Not to me. They have each claimed a piece of me, and I am merely handing over what they demand. *Myself.*

Clothes fly all over my room, landing on the floor and the edges of the bed.

My pulse races from the unknown and the dominance of the two men possessing me. They both know exactly where to touch me, how firm and how soft. Tage remembers the sensitive spot at the nape of my neck, while Alec tickles me right behind my ear with the tip of his tongue.

I sigh and shiver, acclimating to the new universe being born around me.

I stare up at Alec, my heart slowly mending. I never thought he was going to speak to me again, let alone touch me, but his warm look of affection mixed with lust and desire heats my insides. We share a kiss — a steaming, sloppy embrace that rebuilds the pieces of the formally destroyed bridge.

I almost cry. The relief that swells inside me could consume the entire building.

"I thought I lost you," I confess between kisses.

"That's funny, because I thought the same thing." Alec pushes some renegade pieces of hair away from my face as he stares into my eyes.

"I'm not going anywhere," I promise.

"Neither am I."

"Neither am I," Tage chimes in, stealing my face, smothering me with a kiss so hot it sets the curtains on fire.

My entire world is spinning. I've lost track of what's up or down, left or right.

There's only them, and me, and a hotbed of hunger. The merciless want growing more monstrous by the second.

Tage cups both my breasts as he presses his erection into my backside. He moans almost in distress from the friction. "I missed this body." He pinches my nipples, sucking firm kisses all along my neck.

"So what are you going to do about it?" I don't know where the ballsy response comes from, but at the moment, I don't exactly feel like myself.

"So many damn things." Tage throws me onto the mattress, and I land on my back with a little bounce. Both Tage and Alec are kneeling above me, shirtless, pant-less, and breathing fire. The way they're looking at me. The ravenous desire. My skin prickles painfully.

"We're going to make you moan like never before." Alec stalks on top of me, trapping my upper body beneath his. He imprisons my mouth with his as Tage peels my pants then panties away from my hips.

My airway closes as Tage's hot breath caresses my clit. Every part of me is pounding. My head, my ears, my pulse, my pussy. I'm terrified and excited and turned on all at the same time.

"Tell us you want this," Tage croons.

Alec stops kissing me and adds, "Tell us you want both of us."

With clipped breaths and zero control I answer, "Yes. I want this. I want both of you." And it's the God's honest truth. I not only *want* both of them, I *need* both of them. To touch me, to love me, to be with me. To be mine.

I heave crazily at the caress of Tage's tongue. He has my legs pushed widely apart, his palms acting like a joist between my thighs.

"That's it. Moan. It's exactly what we want." Alec adds fuel to the fire, massaging my left breast as he sucks one nipple and then the other into his mouth. Back and forth he goes, all while Tage continually rubs his tongue against my clit. Sensation overload does not even begin to describe it. I can barely move as the two men over-power my body. I want to squirm and wriggle. I want to worm, but I'm trapped. Pinned by pelting sensations of lust and two animal-istic men.

"Oh, fuck." I tense my lower body when Tage slides his tongue deeply into my entrance. "Oh, fuck, oh, fuck, oh, fuck." I pull on Alec's hair as both my nipples and clit pulsate to the same rhythm.

A moment later, there's more blind movement as Tage and Alec switch positions.

Different mouths now eating at my chest and my pussy.

I gasp from the change in pressure and the overwhelming phenomenon. They each have their own unique affect, affection, and affectivity.

Alec slides his tongue through my drenched folds until I'm rocking my hips and begging Tage for more. He just gazes down at me as he gropes my tits, enamored it seems by the strain on my face.

"We're going to give you so much," he promises as Alec sinks a finger slowly inside me. They're torturing me. Drawing out every touch until I feel it so deep it brands my soul. "Tell us how much you want us. Tell us how much you want both of us inside you," Tage cajoles me with a seductive tone.

I didn't think my heart could beat any faster, but I was wrong.

The words "both of us" sends an added shock of stress to my nervous system.

Two men inside me at once?

I grab a fistful of Tage's wild hair, searching his eyes. It's hard to concentrate while Alec French kisses me into oblivion.

"I promised I would always take care of you. This time is no different." He's so in tune to me, it's eerie sometimes. Alec is the only other person on this Earth I connect with in the same way. Maybe that's how we ended up here. On a plane only the three of us can exist on.

I jump as soon as I feel an unexpected pressure down south.

"Relax," Tage calms me, running his lips over my cheek, my eye, and down my nose until they find mine. "You need to stay relaxed and trust us." He applies pressure to my lips as Alec applies pressure to my backside.

"Shit." I squeeze my eyes shut as Alec begins to loosen the tight ring of muscle with his fingers while licking my clit continuously. I wriggle on the bed from the brand-new awareness.

"Stay still, love." Tage pins my hands over my head and kisses me rapturously. I use his mouth as an outlet for stress, nipping and biting at his lips as the waves of bliss hit sharp peaks and steep valleys.

A swipe of Alec's tongue hits an ultra-sensitive spot, and I come with no warning.

I'm electrocuted with pleasure, but he doesn't let up, using the vulnerability of my body to his advantage, to dig deeper, and loosen me even more. I moan senselessly through the orgasm, Tage swallowing my cries as if trying to taste them. Memorize them. Immortalize them.

"Fuck, you're so sweet." He licks his lips.

"I second that." Alec sits up and wipes his mouth like he just devoured a juicy slice of watermelon. "I'm dying for you, baby." He grips his cock, squeezing it tightly.

"I'm right here," I pant nervously, excitedly, more tuned up than I have ever been in my life.

Those are all the words I needed to say.

My bed isn't huge, but it accommodates the three of us just enough. Tage lays on his back, dragging me on top of him. In this position, my ass is beautifully positioned high in the air. I feel Alec saddle up behind me, and I nearly split in two.

Tage traps the cheeks of my face as Alec traps the cheeks of my ass. I feel him rub his erection through my slick folds, lubing himself up with the remnants of my sticky climax.

"You are so fucking wet." He glides against me way too easily. He's right, I am soaked, and needy, and want so much fucking more of the two of them.

"Breathe, Ever," Alec instructs, nudging the head of his cock against me. I suck in air as he works his way into my body, slowly. Sliding in and out inch by tiny inch, stretching me carefully.

I kiss Tage with all my might, absorbing the bites of pain and reveling in the rations of pleasure.

"It will all be worth it," Tage talks me through. "In the end, it will all be worth it."

I tense once Alec is seated halfway inside me. Arching my back, I suddenly feel the urge for more. I want more of him. More of his cock deeper inside me. I push back slightly, and we both moan.

The pain seems to dissipate, and in its place settles a voracious need.

"Alec," I mewl his name, not recognizing my own voice.

"I'm right here," he responds through clenched teeth before jerking his body forward, forcing my eyes to shoot open. He's seated entirely inside me, the length of his erection buried as far as it can go. *Holy fuck, holy fuck, holy fuck.*

The three of us stay utterly still so my body can acclimate to the new intrusion. I stare down at Tage, and once again, he's entranced by the strain on my face.

Alec dots soft kisses on my shoulder blades before rocking his hips slowly. I succumb to the movement of his body, getting lost in the indescribable sensations.

"My turn." Tage runs his hands down my curves and rests them on my hips. He grips me tightly then flexes his pelvis. The first bit of penetration abducts the air right out of my lungs. I gasp as he pushes himself inside, sliding into my channel without any hesitation. He wanted to make a statement. He wanted to shock me. He wanted to hear me moan. He achieved all three.

And fuck, do I moan, I moan so loud I'm positive the people walking by on the busy New York City street hear me.

The satisfaction on his face is smug.

It's the same look from all those years ago, when he knew he was making me feel good.

Tage isn't the only one who wants to make an impression, because as soon as I rebound from his arresting drive, Alec withdraws slightly and thrusts back in. My voice pitches, and the little bit of air I was able to regain is forced right back out of my system.

I'm left a panting mess sandwiched between two governing pillars of sexual authority.

"Don't give up on us yet." Alec slips his hand under my chin and lifts my head. "We're going to come, and so are you." They both begin to move a little more urgently, finding a rhythm that suits all three of us.

The overwhelming fullness has me seeing stars. No, not only stars, constellations, vivid flares, and cosmic rays.

The thought of another orgasm is exhilarating as much as it is terrifying. My first one was so intense and came on so fast I could hardly prepare for it. What will it be like with *two* men pushing me toward the precipice.

"I want you to let it all go." Tage tangles his fingers in my hair, the gyration of his hips keeps his pelvis in constant contact with my clit. It tingles and aches minute after minute, cranking the buildup of my climax from one mindbending level to the next. "All the bad feelings, all the resentment. All the past years of pain," he rasps into my ear. "Leave it all out on the table."

That's a tall order. As much as I love the position we're in now —

physically, mentally, and emotionally — just letting go of the past like it never happened is a new challenge all in itself.

"If you leave me again, you better be dead." Threatening him makes me feel world's better.

Tage chuckles through clenched teeth.

"I promise," he grits out, reveling in my body.

My mind clears of its own accord. I want to let it all go, even if it's just for a few blissful seconds. *Baby steps.*

"I'm here." Alec slides his hand down my chest to massage one of my breasts, reminding me that I'm not alone. That I can lean on him as much as I need.

I don't know how I got here. How I went from no love and no life to an abundance of love and attention in a nanosecond.

For the first time in my life, I feel lucky. Even with the bumps and bruises still fresh from the last couple of days, I somehow walked away from the wreckage better than I have been in years.

I don't know where this will leave the three of us when it's all said and done, but for now I'm going to live in the moment. I'm going to take advantage of what they are offering me and look blindly into the future.

"Make me come," I huff, turning my face back toward Alec. I nip and lick at his lips, and in return he kisses me with a might that's brand new to both of us.

A haze thicker than an Afghanistan sandstorm engulfs us. Lustful demands thin the air and rev our adrenaline, upping the ante.

My body strains from the inside out, every muscle being worked in a whole new way.

Tage and Alec both groan in reaction to the restriction of my inner walls.

It's a sound so sexy I become addicted to it on the spot. I clench tighter, orally fixated on their pleasure.

They both moan again, and my arousal shoots through the roof.

"Fucking Christ." Tage tenses and arches his back as Alec squeezes my breast desperately.

"Ever, I'm too close." Alec bites the shell of my ear. The pain shoots straight to my core. "Let go. Let it all go." It's not a request or a plea — it's a demand. And I know by the tone of his voice he means let go of more than just the physical. And with him by my side, I can. Alec is my strength. He's my trust.

He's the piece that can hold this threesome together.

"Ah!" I erupt, digging my nails into Tage's chest. The climax is coming, and there's no stopping it now.

Rabidly, Tage and Alec tag team to work me over — the push and pull, the in and out — is an out-of-body fucking experience.

The pound of dueling hips and the swell of two cocks has me reeling. Violent convulsions cause both my pussy and ass to clamp, contract, and cramp around both men.

There's an underwater explosion before all the sensations bubble to the surface. It's a frantic, frenzied state of mind that completely takes over, ruling all three of us.

The keening cry that leaves my lips as I come is incommunicable. I can't even believe the sound came from me, but that's how being with both Tage and Alec affects me. It changes me. Rebirths me, revitalizes me. In the end, I'm a brand-new woman. A phoenix. Rising from the ash to face a new day.

Sweaty, sticky, and supremely satisfied, I collapse between Tage and Alec. Nestled between their fiery bodies, the stress of the day drags me away. I couldn't stop the onset of fatigue even if I tried. I'm exhausted, spent, and emotionally drained.

"I love you." It's the last thing I can muster before the darkness steals me away.

I sit on my tiny dresser in a T-shirt and underwear, Denali curled next to me, staring at the two naked men passed out in my bed. Arms and legs hung over the side, they barely fit on the full-sized mattress.

They're both so different. Tage's wild, golden-blond waves are fanned out on the pillow, while Alec's short, styled, dark hair is sticking up on top of his head.

The way they touch me is different. The way they treat me is different. The way they love me is different. Yet, somehow, last night proved that it fits. That we all fit.

It's crazy. This whole scenario is insane. I'm still trying to make sense of it if all. Two men, one woman, one love? One life? Is it really that simple?

Do three lost puzzle pieces come together as easily as that?

I hope beyond hope, because last night changed everything. Now that I have them both, I can't let either go.

It may just break me.

"How long are you going to sit there and stare?" Tage asks randomly with his eyes still closed.

"How long have you been up?" I counter.

"I never went to sleep."

"I've been sitting here for quite a while." I watched the sun come up.

"I know." His facial muscles don't move, but I swear he grimaced through his tone.

"You're way too good of an actor," I accuse.

"Comes with the job description." He pops one gorgeous, hazel eye open.

I'm not amused. I don't want him acting around me.

"Come back to bed." He reaches a hand out. "That sour expression is going to give you wrinkles."

"Since when do you care about wrinkles?"

"I don't, but it sounded good."

I laugh. *Idiot.*

"Hey." Alec pops his head up and rests on his forearms. "If we're gonna do this, we're investing in a bigger bed."

My face splits with a smile. "Are we really going to do this?" I ask the question that has been burning a hole in my brain all morning.

"Why not? What's that old saying? Two dicks are better than one?"

I crack up. "I don't think that's the saying."

"It can be our saying. Now get your ass back to bed," Alec orders.

I relent. There is no place I would rather be than trapped between those two men.

I scurry across my small room and hop into bed, landing right between them. Neither of them hesitates for a second to put their hands or lips on me, each claiming a piece of my body for themselves.

"I haven't seen you naked in eight years. Don't ever put clothes on again." Tage rips my T-shirt right off me.

"Food shopping might be an issue."

"We can order in." He attacks my neck while Alec drags hot kisses across my abdomen.

"It's going to be a long day, isn't it?" I moan.

"Yes," they answer in tandem.

21

T age

A FUCKFEST IS EXACTLY what I needed.

It's exactly what Everly and I both needed. Sex may not be the answer to all our problems, but it sure helps to relieve some serious stress.

I towel dry my hair then wrap the pink terry cloth around my waist. I inspect myself in the mirror. I need a serious haircut. I pull the wavy strands straight up through my fingers. Four inches too long, at least.

Everly doesn't seem to mind the length. She was pulling the shit out it every chance she got. I smile at the memory.

Whatever makes her happy. And whatever gets her off.

I stroll out of the bathroom to find Everly and Alec half dressed in her barely there kitchen. I got her this place when she first moved to the city. Decent neighborhood, rent-controlled, and fairly spacious for New York. It was just one of the many ways I tried to take care of her. I have always just wanted to take care of her.

Ever is sitting on the counter with an open container of chocolate hazelnut spread. I swear she can eat that shit by the gallon. Alec is teasing her, dotting chocolate on her nose and cheeks, then licking it off. She's giggling like a child. Like a carefree child, and for some reason, the sound hits me square in the chest. It's like I can feel it. Feel her happiness. It's . . . uncomfortable. I spent most of my life suppressing my feelings. Walking around numb so I could do my job. But Everly has always managed to break through the barrier. There isn't anything I wouldn't do for her, including sharing her with the other man she loves.

I could never take that smile away from her. Not again, because once upon a time, she smiled at me exactly like that.

"Take a ten-minute shower and I miss all the fun." I walk over and stick my finger in the jar.

"We were just buying time until you got done," Everly flirts.

"Well, I'm done." I suck the chocolate off my finger then give her a firm, sugary kiss.

"I noticed." She exhales, lightheaded.

"Dinner should be here in a little while. I ordered from this fantastic Mexican place uptown." Alec smiles, then it fades. "Guess I should have asked if you like Mexican."

Yeah, it's definitely apparent there are going to be a lot of "get to know you" moments in the immediate future. Alec and I may have Everly in common, but who the hell knows what else? Maybe nothing. From the little I know about him, definitely nothing. He's a high-powered, hoity-toity lawyer who likes the finer shit in life, and I'm an undercover nomad who doesn't exist on paper. And I couldn't care less about the finer shit in life. All I need is a bed, a shirt, a gun, and I'm all good.

This mix should be interesting.

"Tage?" Everly waves her hand in front of my face. "Whata'ya thinkin' about? You got scary quiet there for a second."

I shake off my internal analysis. "Just hoping the guac is good."

Everly arches an eyebrow. She's questioning my bullshit. It seems Alec shares her suspicions, but he doesn't care enough to question me, too.

Alec and I are going to have to have one serious heart to heart. Just the two of us. Mano y mano.

He looks pretty on the outside, but I get the feeling Mr. Alec M. Prescott, Esquire, doesn't mind getting dirty one bit.

"Ever," I address her seriously. "There is something all three of us need to discuss over dinner." I hate to be the party pooper, but there is still the issue of her mother, what she wants, and exactly what lengths she's willing to go to get it.

For the last several years, Vicki has been off the grid, popping up here and there when she tanked out of rehab or ended up in jail. I've always kept tabs on her and Gunner, but this recent appearance has me concerned. It looks like she has some money and power behind her, but I can't be completely sure. It could all be an act. I'm going to find out either way. And I'm going to keep Everly as far away from her as possible while I do.

"About what my mom wants?" She was never a stupid girl.

"Yes. You said you might know?"

She chews on her lip. With her hair a mess and the freckles on her nose, she looks like a scared little girl. But she's anything but. Her appearance doesn't reflect the person inside. It never has. I often wondered if that's why Gunner was so obsessed with her. He saw how rare she was. As fragile as a petal on the outside but as fierce as a lion within.

"I heard them fighting that night. Before everything happened. Outside my bedroom door. My mom, she was screaming about a key. That she wanted it. It belonged to her, not him," Everly recalls painfully. The scrunch of her nose and dimples between her eyebrows scrape at my heart. "She sounded crazy. Not that that was too far off for my mom. She was always a little unstable, but she was extra upset that night."

"And what was Gunner saying?"

"Not much, just yelling, 'Shut up, bitch. You're high.' But I heard her say 'key' clearly. She wanted a key."

"A key?" I pace the tiny kitchen. "Key to what?" I wonder aloud, racking my brain. It was a long time ago, but I don't remember Gunner ever mentioning any kind of key or lock box or car. What else can a key be used for?

"Tage?" Everly calls my name, worried.

"I'm just thinking."

"What I want to know is why she approached me?" Alec chimes in. "If she wants Everly so badly, why go through all the trouble to use me? Why not just grab her and be done with it?"

"Because just grabbing her would gain too much attention. *My* attention. But grab both her and her boyfriend. They could do a lot with that."

"How?" Alec is pessimistic.

"Manipulating social media, for one. Create an alibi for the two of you. Pretend to be on vacation? A romantic getaway. Who would question that?"

"Our bosses, for one," Everly scoffs.

"Maybe, but that's the least of Vicki's worries. Once she had you, and then got what she wanted, neither of you would go back to work, I'm sure," I insinuate the inevitable. A six-foot-deep ditch in the ground and two warm bodies.

A phone begins to ring, and we all pause. "That's probably dinner." Alec swipes his phone off the coffee table and then curses. *I don't think it's dinner.*

"Who is it?" I rush over to him.

"Her." He holds up the screen. Caller unknown flashes.

"What do we do?" Everly directs the question right at me.

"Don't answer it. Let her call. She's not getting anywhere near any of us."

The buzzer rings, and Everly nearly jumps through the roof. "Relax." I place my hands on her arms and try to soothe her as Alec answers the door.

"I thought this was over," she nearly cries.

"Me, too, but I'm here, and I'll end it once and for all. I promise."

Everly nods as the smell of warm spices fills the room.

"You need to eat something." Alec places a kiss on her neck as he walks by.

"I'm not hungry."

"Don't let her get in your head." I shake her lightly.

"How can I not? She has done nothing but ruin my life, and now she's back for more. To do more damage. To take away the first shred of real happiness I've had in a long time."

Jesus, she's killing me.

"She's not going to take a goddamn thing." Alec steps behind Everly so we are sandwiching her body. "*We* won't let anything happen to you or your happiness." Alec looks directly over Everly's head and straight into my eyes. He's communicating to both me and her. I nod in agreement. She's ours, and we'll both protect her in our own ways. "Your mom doesn't intimidate me." He tilts her chin up. "And whatever it is she thinks you have, she can just try to come fucking get it."

"She threatened you. Your career."

"Who gives a fuck about my career? I can be a lawyer anywhere. There is only one you. One us. That's more important than anything."

I stare at Alec as he gazes down at Everly. His lip is still a little swollen from our roll around yesterday, and his hair is messy from an earlier shower. At the moment, he looks more street than superior legal counsel, and for some reason, my respect for him grows. He's formidable. Much tougher on the inside than he looks on the out, which is exactly who I need in my corner right now.

Vicki has a knack for getting wrapped up with the worst kind of people, and I'm positive she isn't working alone.

"What do we do?" Everly asks into the void.

There's only one thing to do.

"Tap the source," I foretell.

22

E verly

When Tage said we needed to go see Gunner, I nearly shit. Go see the man who locked me away from the world for three years? Who kept me prisoner in his house like an animal in the zoo?

It was a fight, to say the least. I thought my past was behind me. Way behind me, but I realize now it's not. It never will be, not with my mother walking around society freely or Gunner living out his days in jail.

After Tage made several phone calls to God only knows who, and three ignored calls from my mother by Alec, we are boarding a private jet in New Jersey headed straight back to the heart of darkness. The place I grew up and hoped never to return to again. Chicago.

I'm antsy, distressed, and a little disturbed. This plane ride is going to be two hours of sheer hell.

"You're so tense you're giving *me* knots." Alec massages my shoulders as we climb the jet stairs.

"I can't help it. I don't want to see him. I don't want any of this. I just want to go back to bed," I complain.

"And hide under the covers with Tage and me?"

"Yes, exactly that."

"Soon enough, baby." He kisses the top of my head. "When this is all over, you're barely going to be able to climb off the mattress," he promises.

"Hoorah!" Tage agrees.

"Service man?" Alec asks as we step inside the spacious jet. Jesus, this thing is a house with wings.

"Army brat all my life. Spent a little time in, too, before I was recruited for bigger and badder things." He winks, clicking his tongue.

I take a seat on the plush leather couch beside the windows. It's big enough for all three of us to sit. Tage and Alec both claim a spot beside me, trapping me in like I've noticed they like to do. How strange has my life become? Loved by two men who are completely content sharing me? I steal looks at them both, and true to their perceptive nature, they both notice.

"Something on your mind, Ever?" Tage asks.

"A million things," I reply.

"Want to share a few?" Alec inquires.

"I wouldn't even know where to begin."

"Getting used to the new dynamic?" Tage offers.

"Yes," I confirm. "Is this completely crazy? The three of us?"

"Yes." Alec barks a laugh. "It's insane. But it also feels right." He lays his hand over mine. "And we want you to be happy."

"I am happy." I can barely believe it. My heart is filled with more love than I ever dreamed capable.

"That's all that matters." Tage slips his arm around my shoulders.

"I want both of you to be happy." This all can't be about me. If it is, it will implode with disaster in the end.

Tage and Alec share a look. I wish I could read their minds. "We're happy," Tage puts my fears to rest.

"Trust us," Alec smirks wickedly.

"I'm placing all my trust in the two of you." The plane begins to taxi, and my insides wobble like Jell-O.

I close my eyes and breathe deeply. I can do this. As long as I have them, I can do this.

"I'll die before I let you down again," Tage pledges.

"Yeah, and I'll kill him if he hurts you," Alec threatens.

"You could try," Tage scoffs.

"And succeed." Alec just has to have the last word. I should warn Tage, arguing with a lawyer is a waste of time. He should conserve his energy for more important things. I've seen Alec in a courtroom. He'll suck the life right out of him.

Tage just laughs Alec off as he gets comfortable, resting his head back on the top edge of the sofa. "I'm beginning to like you way more than I thought I was going to."

"Once you get past his asshole exterior, he's pretty awesome," I feel compelled to comment.

"Thank you so much for the compliment." Alec peers down at me pretending to be miffed.

"You're welcome." I smile sweetly.

He rolls his eyes, but I know he isn't mad. He's fully aware he's an asshole sometimes, and that's just the way he likes it.

Once we're in the air, we unbuckle our seatbelts, and Tage attacks the mini fridge.

"Snacks?" He pulls out three different types of candy, soda, water, and some small bottles of rum.

I go straight for the alcohol. Because why the hell not? I crack it open and down the whole thing.

"Easy, killer." Tage chuckles.

"I need something to take the edge off." I stand up and start pacing the plane.

"Relax," he tells me yet again, but I can't. I wasn't prepared for any of this. Not the two of them, or my mother, or a road trip to see Gunner.

I lift a curtain toward the back of the plane and come upon another room. A bedroom. Fancy. Looks like a queen-sized bed and enough room for two end tables on each side.

"Tage? Whose plane is this again?" I voice.

"Endeavor's. They own all kinds of fun toys."

Fun toys? I eye the neatly made bed. Maybe that's exactly what I need to relax. A little fun, with two of my toys.

"Did you know there's a bedroom back here?" I pop out of the curtain.

Tage shrugs. "Sometimes we fly far."

"Is that all it's used for? Sleeping?" I pull my T-shirt over my head. Both Tage and Alec freeze.

"I'm sure it's been utilized for other things." Tage watches me intently, like a cat stalking a mouse.

"Have you ever used it for other things?" I unbutton my jean shorts and slide them down my legs.

"I haven't . . . yet."

I turn around and glance over my shoulder at them as I lift the curtain. "You two coming, or are you going to leave me to my own devices?"

Tage and Alec both spring to their feet, pushing and shoving each other in a race to get to me first.

"Leave you to your own devices?" Alec gives me a little shove onto the bed. "No. But we'd be more than happy to watch you play with *your devices* first." They both stand over the mattress with me half-naked and horny.

"I'll touch myself, but I want you to take your clothes off while I do." A double strip tease? Yes, please.

There's not one ounce of hesitation on either of their parts. Eyeing me like two starving wolves, I slide my hand into my panties and massage myself until my cheeks begin to heat.

"If we're getting naked, so are you." Tage rips the black silky material away from my hips. They have a bird's-eye view of my bare pussy now. Just how they want it.

I tease myself, using just the tip of my middle finger to circle the dewy pink flesh.

My inner thighs quiver as I pleasure myself all while watching two of the hottest men I've ever laid eyes on strip away each piece of their clothing. They're styles are starkly different. Alec pulls off a polo shirt and a pair of khaki shorts while Tage discards a beat-up t-shirt and worn jeans. Both so different and yet so equally hot.

"Oh," I moan as my clit aches. The altitude, the temperature, and the arousal are going straight to my head.

Both men lose their underwear at the same time, and it is now an even playing field.

"Don't stop touching yourself." Alec climbs onto the mattress and drops his head between my legs. Using his tongue, he follows my ministrations, chasing after the path my fingers are taking.

"Oh, God," I mewl as the added pressure and smooth caress adds fuel to the kindling fire.

Tage watches as together Alec and I both work my body over. We make eye contact, a flaming connection linking the two of us. He jerks his shaft slowly, possessed by the show.

I'm possessed, too. By the two men who are about to ravish me. I want them to make me forget. Forget about the past, the present, and the all the unknowns of the future. I want them to seize my mind and force me to think about only them. About only us. The three of us.

"Flip her over." Tage's voice is husky as hell. It sends shivers straight to the tips of each of my fingers and toes.

I know what's coming. Both of these men each own a part of me. I gave Tage one version of my virginity all those years ago, and Alec another just last night. They were each a first of mine in their own way. And once they claimed their piece, they spent most of the day trading off, indulging in one another's possession.

Alec flips me onto my stomach before pulling me onto all fours. My heart hammers and so does every inch of my lower body. Fuck, I want them. Both of them. At the same time. Touching me, kissing, fucking me.

Alec repositions himself back underneath me, his mouth returning to the same place it just left. I moan loudly as his tongue invades my entrance. God, that feels beyond amazing.

"That's it, baby, get nice and wet for us. Just how we like you."

Gladly. I grind against Alec's face, thriving in all the attention.

I feel Tage's hands rest on my ass cheeks and quiver. Four hands and one common ground are incredible odds.

"Excited, are we?" Tage teases me. God, fucking yes, I am. I'm fucking addicted to both these men. I fell hard and fast and blindly into the darkness, and now it owns me. It controls me. It dominates me. It takes away all good reason and leaves me floating in the barbaric black.

"Touch me," I plead, jutting my hips back toward him.

Alec bites my clit and I yelp. "I'm not through with you."

"I'm sorry." I ease back onto his face, allowing his mouth to ravage me once again.

He groans as he wraps his arms around my thighs and eats away at my pussy. I'm trapped now, in a vulnerable position. A position Tage takes full advantage of.

I feel the dip of his finger inside my soaked entrance and the trace of the slick tip around my exposed button hole. I breathe heavily, fighting to keep my bearings as he penetrates me skull-splittingly slow.

Fuck.

"So fucking sweet," he hums as he fingers me. I pant, fighting not to come. Everything down south compresses, the pressure building monumentally, minute by painstaking minute.

The two of them work as a skilled team to keep me wet and relax my tight muscles.

Alec licking and sucking, while Tage dips and fingers both my holes, sometimes simultaneously.

When he's able to stretch three fingers inside me, I'm ready. Ready for him. Ready for him to take me. For them both to take me.

"Alec, Tage," I whine desperately when I feel the tip of Tage's cock breech my entrance.

"Keep breathing, baby." Tage fights his way into my body, his fingertips digging into my hip bones. In and out in small, punchy thrusts, he breaks me like a wild horse. "Fuck. Mine," he heaves once he's fully seated inside. My muscles adjust, contracting around his cock.

"Mine, too." Alec slides his way up my body, dragging his tongue along my torso as he goes. Once he reaches my chest, he doesn't even bother unhooking my bra, he just rips the material down so my tits pop out. He sucks and licks each nipple keenly as he guides the head of his erection to my wanton pussy.

Yes, yes, yes, I internally chant as he drives inside me. For a split second, I black out from the bliss. There's no feeling remotely close to those first few moments of overwhelming fullness or the several split seconds of euphoric force that's like a semiconductor frying my brain.

The urge to come is catastrophic. Each of us contributing to a chorus of animalistic sounds. Alec kisses me as he thrusts inside me, the taste of my arousal is potent on his lips.

The embrace doesn't last as Tage yanks on my hair, breaking our embrace, savagely burying himself to the hilt.

"You're so tight." Tage clenches jaw. "And wet." Alec punches again, and I scream from the ungodly pressure and compulsion to come.

"I'm so close," I cry, panting like crazy person. My back is as slick with sweat as my pussy is with desire.

"Ride us." Tage stops moving. "Ride us both until you come." It's quiet in my head for a fraction of a second as they ease up on me, both slowing to almost a halt.

I am finally able to open my eyes, and when I do, I find Alec staring back at me, irises more electric than a current.

"Come. Come all over me," he heaves, expression untamed.

I have no other choice than to give in to his request. I want to come more than anything. And I want them both inside me when I do.

I move awkwardly at first, searching for the right rhythm, but when I finally find it, it's a powerhouse of pleasure.

I fuck them both in a seesaw-like motion until my body is splitting. Until my heart is pounding, my tendons are tearing, and my inner walls are constricting so tightly I cut off the blood supply to Tage's and Alec's cocks.

I crack, coming so hard tears actually escape down my cheeks. The altitude combined with the bodily rush thins my intake of air right before I lose control of all bodily functions, climaxing at the peak of our crowning point. A mishmash of hands, lips, and tongues accompany our climatic journey. I lose track of what happens next as the white noise takes over. Stealing my sight and every sound.

Gradually, I recover from the bombing as the man above me and the man below me rebound from their own release.

A domino effect ensues, I collapse on Alec and Tage collapses on me. The three of us exhausted, physically taxed, and completely spent.

I still don't know how this became my life, but I wouldn't change it, sell it, or trade it for anything in the entire world.

It's late by the time we get to the hotel. My mother has called Alec six times, and he has ignored each call under Tage's direction. My destressor has worn off, and I am back to being high-strung. I have no idea how I'm going to sleep tonight. Just the thought of seeing Gunner in the morning . . . . My stomach flip-flops. I was never a huge fan of him, even as a child. He was just creepy. Always looking at me with those dark, shifty eyes. When he decided to rip away my freedom, my dislike grew by leaps and bounds, morphing straight into hatred. I still get hives just thinking about that room, the locked door, the loneliness, the despair. I was dying. Wasting away until the day I met Tage.

He saved me in so many ways.

I stare at the lights of downtown Chicago from the luxurious hotel room. The Riverwalk below is bustling with people and twinkling with life. It's strange being back here. I never thought I'd return. Yet, here I am, with the past hot on my heels.

"Whatcha lookin' at out there?" Alec leans on the window next to me.

"I'm looking at a lifetime's worth of pain and suffering."

"I'm sorry for that." He inches closer and cups my chin, swiping his thumb back and forth across my cheek.

"I thought it was all behind me."

"It will be."

"Alec, I'm sorry."

"For what?"

"Dragging you into my shit. Into all my problems."

"You didn't drag me into anything. You didn't know."

"I didn't. And if I did, I would have stayed away."

"I wouldn't have let you. Shit or not, I want to be with you. In a short amount of time, you have given me so much. Changed so much. We'll get through this. And it'll be you and me on the other side." He pauses, considering something. "You, me, and Tage," he corrects.

I look at Alec with so much love and admiration in my heart. He is so strong. So confident. Totally cocky. And he loves me unconditionally even though there is another man in my life. *How did I get so fucking lucky? How did this happen?* I'm still trying to figure it out. I just know every second that ticks by, I'm bonded to these two men in inexplicable ways. They are quickly

becoming the foundation of my lifeforce.

"I love you," I declare softly.

"I love you more." Alec kisses me gently, sweetly, wholeheartedly, earnestly.

I sigh against his mouth.

I can do this. As long as he's here, I can do anything.

23

T age

THE SOUND of running water wakes me up.

Alec is knocked out on his side of the king-sized bed and Everly is missing.

I find her standing under the spray, hair soaked, arms crossed. Her gaze is distant and the look of her breaks me apart.

"It's a little late for a shower." I open the glass door and she jumps from surprise.

"I couldn't sleep."

"Want some company?"

Everly shrugs.

I drop my drawers and step into the steaming shower. Christ Almighty, the water's hot. So much so her skin is scalding red.

"Jesus, baby," I turn the temperature of the water down slightly.

"You're going to give yourself third degree burns." I touch her chest lightly.

"Huh?" She looks down at herself. "I didn't even feel it."

"So I noticed."

"I didn't mean to wake you."

"I don't mind. I don't sleep much anyway." I run my fingers through her hair, loving the softness of the strands.

I never really got to touch her. To just explore in a slow, appreciative way.

"What are you looking at, Tage?" She notices the way I trap the ends of her dark hair between my fingers.

"You should stop dying your hair."

I have always thought that. Since the first time she did it. "Your natural color is so much prettier."

"It's red." She curls her lip. She was never a fan.

"It's auburn, and it's beautiful. Complements your freckles." I follow the pattern of dots across her nose with one fingertip. "You're a rare beauty. Embrace it."

She stares up at me silently, the echo of the water pouring down around us.

"Did you always think that?" she asks meekly.

"That you're a rare beauty? Yes. From the moment I saw you. I never stopped thinking it. I never stopped thinking about you."

"I never stopped thinking about you either." She traces the face of my ferocious dragon tattoo. It wasn't there when we were together. I got it a few years later. To cover the scar Gunner left when he shot me and as a symbol of strength. Of survival. Of endurance.

A reminder, I'm not so easy to kill. That mindset takes you a long way in my line of work.

"I know you didn't." I cover her hand with mine. Everything has been so crazy over the last few days. Moving so fast there has barely been time to breathe. To take it all in. We needed a chance to reconnect, just the two of us, and we're finally getting it.

Everly explores my body with her hands, dragging her fingertips slowly over my torso and stopping at the angry blue koi tattoo on my hip bone. That was there when we were together. She drinks me in, and for the first time in what feels like forever there's

no barrier between us.

I've been watching her through glass for eight long years, we could always see each other, but I was on the outside looking in and she was on the inside looking out. Total separation and complete awareness all at the same time.

Sheer torture.

Her fingers move a little lower and I quiver. "Keep touching me like that and something dirty is bound to happen."

"What's wrong with that?" Her words are soft, seductive, not laced with lust, but filled with emotion.

"Nothing. Nothing's wrong with that." I take her face and kiss her emotively. "But that's not why I came in here."

"Maybe that's exactly what I need. Just you. Right here, right now."

"Love, you can have me any time, any way you want me. I'm here for whatever you need. Always."

It's a pledge. One I took long ago when I fell in love with a young, innocent girl who burrowed her way right under my skin and straight into my heart.

Everly kisses me, and it's the most honest embrace of my life. It's pure, and unspoiled and belongs solely to us.

I lift her off the ground and pin her to the wall, just so I can get closer. So every part of us can connect. We do nothing but kiss. Do nothing but stroke our tongues and set our inhibitions free.

I don't know how long it goes on for, the heady kissing and the outpour of love, but both our bodies react to the connection. Succumb to the inevitable. The constant rub of my erection against her pussy puts us on a one-way path.

"Tage." My name falls from Everly's lips, and the innocent word destroys me.

With one tiny lift of her hips I'm sinking inside her, taking everything she's offering me.

"Fuck, I love you." I move slowly, gluttonously, absorbing each generous inch of her body.

"I love you, too," she huffs as that's what we partake in, a head-on collision of love.

Everly jerks up the wall with each of my powerful thrusts. The punches of pleasure evident on her gorgeous face.

"Tage," she moans freely, and I eat it fucking up. How long have I waited for this? For us?

I continue with my measured strokes, bracing for impact. It's coming — we both are.

"Oh, fuck," Everly pants with her eyes squeezed shut. She's strangling the shit out of my cock, forcing my hips to move faster.

"Damn," I choke as she comes. She's so free, so alive, and it's all because of me. I watch her for as long as I can, body plastered against the shower wall, riding a tidal wave of ecstasy.

Finally, I implode, throbbing harder and roaring louder than I could even anticipate. This wasn't a hard, fast fuck, that drummed up my adrenaline faster than the speed of sound. It was a passionate, painstaking affair that employed every part of us. The physical, the mental, the spiritual.

I crush her against the wall with my body, heaving for air. Everly buries her face in my neck and we just are.

We are just there. Just together. Just satisfied. Just content. Just ready to face whatever the future has in store.

24

I DON'T KNOW if Everly is up for this.

I'm wracked with indecision just looking at her. She may be calm on the outside but she's a freaking mess on the inside.

I prepare witnesses for trial for a living, I know the signs. I can see when they are going to crack. And I think this pressure might just be Ever's undoing.

She wrings her hands in the back seat of the SUV as we drive out to Chicago Statesville Penitentiary. It's where Gunner is serving twenty-five to life for aggravated assault, child endangerment, drug trafficking, and attempted murder. Bad dude pretty much sums him up. It's no wonder Ever is wound tighter than a guitar string.

"Here." I hand her my vape from the front seat. "It will take the edge off."

Without missing a beat, she grabs the pen and takes a hard

drag. She chokes right after, coughing her head off. Everly has never been interested in smoking or doing any kind of drug that I'm aware of. Ramifications of a drug-addict mother, I'm sure. Every time I puffed, she just let me do my thing. Because it was just that, my thing. She takes another lungful, and this time she manages to handle it better. The car smells like blueberries now, thanks to my new choice in oil. Everly hands the pen back, and I take a pull myself, expelling a thick cloud of smoke out the cracked window. I offer it to Tage next. We can just make it a puff-puff party.

He grabs the pen and mimics my actions, his cloud of smoke rivaling mine.

The car becomes quiet after that. Each of us lost in our own unique high.

Which is, I think, what we all needed. Calm and quiet before the storm.

TAGE PULLED some strings to get us in to see Gunner. Whatever organization he works for, it has deep pockets and a hell of a far reach. Since we left New York, the dime has been on them. The hotel room, the car, the food, and now this. A private escort straight to a notorious criminal. And I thought I worked for high rollers.

We are met at the gate by two corrections officers and the warden himself. *Damn.*

We all exchange the necessary niceties. Introductions, handshakes, and all that, then we are walking. Through maximum security hallways that are a dusty yellow and direly depressing.

Remind me never to commit any felonies.

Ever is a spooked cat. Both Tage and I remain close, flanking each side of her like bodyguards. That's what we'll both become, too, if it comes down to it.

We are shown into a medium-sized room with a table and several chairs. The windows overhead are grimy, and there is a faint smell of bleach and piss.

Yum.

"He's being escorted now," the warden informs us. He's a well-dressed man in a blue suit with calluses on his hands and weathered lines around his eyes.

"I appreciate the assistance." Tage shakes his hand once again.

"Officer Shipman and Officer Foreman will assist you with anything further. Don't hesitate to contact me."

"Will do," Tage agrees. He's been different since we stepped out of the car. Overly serious, professional, and quite frankly, a bit fucking intimidating. I'm impressed.

He's showing me he's more than just a lone cowboy.

The warden leaves, Officers Shipman and Foreman adopt a position in each corner of the room. Everly nearly expires in her seat, and Tage paces. It's tension fucking city in the twelve-by-twelve enclosure.

I sit next to Everly and take her hand, passing her an encouraging smile. She looks like she wants to puke.

There's a knock on the steel door, and the roller coaster begins. A moment later, a man shackled in irons with tattoos all over his neck and one teardrop by his eye dressed in dark grey scrubs is escorted in by two corrections officers who look like they compete in body-building competitions as a side job. I have been to plenty of jails, visited numerous kinds of inmates, but this is a whole new level even for me.

The guards sit Gunner down and attach his handcuffs to the link on the tabletop. I muster my most stoic face as Gunner runs his black eyes over each of us. He clearly has no idea what he's here for.

When they land on Tage, he smirks darkly. "You're still walking around, groundhog?"

Groundhog?

"Loud and proud." Tage doesn't cower.

"How many of those nine lives you got left?" It almost sounds like a threat.

"Enough." Tage's response mirrors Gunners. It's clear they have history. I did a little research on Gunner and the raid that went down at his compound eight years ago. Of all the agencies mentioned, Endeavor was not one of them, and there was no mention of an operative named Tage, not even in the court files I could access.

It was quite the takedown, though. Millions of dollars in cash and drugs were seized, along with militarized assault weapons. Gunner had his hands in a little bit of everything. Including child abuse and neglect.

Everly is so eerily quiet I almost forget she's in the room. She has somehow managed to shrink away to nothing, to near invisibility.

Gunner sees her, though. I have a feeling she was never invisible to him.

"You are so grown up." He almost sounds nostalgic. She remains silent. "Why you here, pretty? Never thought I'd see you again."

"I didn't want to come." Everly's voice is gravelly.

"But here you are, with . . .?" He finally notices me. "Who the hell are you?"

"Legal counsel," is my snarky reply.

"Legal counsel? *Right*." Gunner knows there's more to me than that. Five minutes in his presence and I can already tell he's shrewd, intelligent, and greasier than motor oil.

He looks around the room, at me, at Tage, at Everly. "What exactly is going on here? What's this all about?"

"Mom," Everly provides him with the answer.

"Aww, Christ. Is she dead?"

"I wish."

Ouch.

"What's she up to now?"

"Trying to ruin my life. *Again*."

"This time I have nothin' to do with it. I'm vacationing here." He lifts his bound wrists and the metal clinks.

"You know the funny thing about the past, Gunner?" Tage plants his hands on the tabletop and leans over. "It has a shitty way of coming back to haunt you."

Gunner's eyes sharpen. "Don't get too close, groundhog. I still bite."

"So do I," Tage hisses.

"Stop." Everly slams her palms on the table. "Please just fucking stop." Everyone's attention lands on her. She looks up at Tage, nearly ready to crack. "He almost killed you once."

"*Almost* being the operative word. He can't do shit now." Tage has balls of steel. I'm forming a new kind of respect for him.

"Can't I?" Gunner grunts.

"You threatening me in the presence of a high-powered lawyer and a room full of officers?"

"I'm not threatening shit. Just protecting my ego." Gunner stays calm, but we all know how much malice is behind his words.

"Gunner," Everly huffs. "I heard you and my mom fighting over some key. I think she's after it now. Where is it, and what's it for?" Everly's done playing. She wants answers, and she wants to get the hell out of here. I stealthily place my hand on her thigh for support. No one but Tage can see.

Gunner's black eyes narrow. He's a scary motherfucker. I will not lie. His buzzed head, tattoos, sharp cheekbones, and gold crowned tooth scream street king.

"I don't recall ever fighting about a key. Got no idea what you're talking about."

"You're lying," I call him out. I can read the signs even if they're all subtle. Gunner is an expert liar, but I still catch the twitch of his finger, the heavy bob of his Adam's apple, and tick of his jaw. Reading people is what I do. What I'm paid to do, and I do it real fucking well.

"I can't help you, pretty." Gunner never takes his eyes off me as he addresses Ever. "Got no clue. Your mama is a wild one. Devil only knows what's happening in that drug sick head of hers."

"What a fucking waste." Everly shoots out of her chair, sending it

flying backwards to the floor "You ruined my life. You stole everything from me. *Why? What for?* What was I worth?"

I think those questions have been festering for years. Even if we
don't find out what Vicki is after, confronting Gunner might be a
type of closure Everly needs.

"I loved you like a daughter."

"You are incapable of love," she spits. All the men in the room
crowd her, including myself.

"You deserve death. You and my mother." For a split second, I
think Gunner is actually hurt. Maybe on some warped, twisted level
he did care for her.

Tage and I begin to drag Everly out of the room. She's had
enough. She's upset and agitated and fighting like hell not to cry. She
wants to be strong. She doesn't want Gunner to see her tears. I realize
in the heat of the moment that she has been suffering for so long.
More than I can even comprehend.

"Destiny," Gunner calls, and she cringes at her birth name.
"You're worth as much as a single fingerprint."

We all look at Gunner like he's crazy. What in the hell is that
supposed to mean?

"I know what a single fingerprint is worth. *Nothing.*" Everly
storms out of the room.

Well, that was a total fucking waste of time and energy.

"He was a fucking kook then, and he's a fucking kook now." She
stomps down the hallway. "Always talking in riddles that make no
damn sense."

I glance over at Tage inquisitively, keeping pace with Everly.

"I don't know." He shakes his head. "Gunner always came out
with weird shit like that. He loved to play head games," Tage
explains.

Wonderful. Someone could have warned me we were going to
see the Riddler.

"Why did you think this was a good idea, Tage?" Everly spins
on her heel once we're back outside. She's clearly upset and unravel-

ling at the seams. "We should have known he wouldn't give us answers."

"Who said he didn't give us answers?" Tage argues, and she looks at him like he's looney. We both do. "Gunner is one of the smartest criminals I have ever encountered. He left us a clue."

"About fingerprints, and how much they're fucking worth?"

"Maybe, and maybe one about you."

"What are you thinking?" I ask Tage, intrigued.

"Nothing solid at the moment, but there is a reason Gunner locked you away. My gut has always told me that. More than it being a freaky obsession."

"You know what I think? It's all just more bullshit. Gunner is bored. So he sends us off to stew over a riddle that has no answer. He has no clue what my mom wants. If you wanted to get to the source of the problem, we should have confronted *her*."

"Gunner was the much safer option," Tage disagrees. "He's incarcerated. Less chance of bullets flying."

"A bullet flying in her direction doesn't sound so bad to me."

"One flying in your direction does." Tage opens the car door for her. Everly jumps in, sprawling out across the back seat.

"Maybe we should set up a meeting?" I suggest to Tage. "Just me and you. Find out what she's after."

"Hell no." Everly pops her head up. "Tage, can't you just have her arrested or deported to another country or something?"

"One, I can't arrest people. I'm not a cop. Two, I can't deport a US citizen, as much as I would like to. Three, she hasn't broken any laws."

"She threatened Alec!"

"I have no solid proof. Only hearsay. She won't be held."

"Ugh. Are you sure you're not a cop? Because you sound just like one."

"I'm just familiar with the law."

"I, unfortunately, can confirm everything he just said," I add.

"This is a nightmare." Everly drops back down, defeated.

"It's a bump in the road. We'll figure it out."

"Can we stop and buy out a liquor store on the way back to the hotel? I think I'm going to need a liquid dinner."

"We can stop for a bottle or two."

"It better be the good stuff. One hundred plus proof."

"Sure," Tage pacifies her.

"Tage, Alec?" Everly's tone is meek.

"Mmmm?" I look back at Ever as Tage drives.

"Promise me I never have to come back to Chicago again."

Tage and I exchange a look. "No, never," I promise on behalf of both of us.

"Good." She closes her eyes and laces her hands over her stomach. She sort of looks like she's laid out in a coffin. It makes me shiver.

A life without Ever?

Unimaginable.

25

E verly

I DRINK my weight's worth of tequila.

Alec bought the really good stuff. Strong and smooth. Deceptive it's even alcohol.

Seeing Gunner again twisted my sanity into a goddamn pretzel, and now I'm trying to deal.

Since we got back the hotel, Tage has been on the phone with God knows who, and Alec has been surfing the Internet. Both on a mission to decode Gunner's riddle. It's a waste of time. There's no answer. They're both dogs chasing their tails.

I'm doing the only productive thing. Getting drunk.

"I'm going to bed." I slink off the couch. I'm tired and tipsy and ready to pass out.

"Sleep on your stomach," Alec advises with his eyes plastered to the screen.

"Promise." I hold up scout's honor.

"We'll be in later." Tage drops a kiss on my head. I smile faintly. The only good thing that came out of all this is sharing a fancy hotel room with the two of them.

"I love you," I hum. "Both of you."

"We love you right back," Tage returns as I step into the bedroom. The mattress is calling.

I fall face first like Alec advised. See? I listen. I close my eyes and sink into the plushy comforter.

Tequila, take me away.

I WAKE UP EARLY, starving, and dying of thirst.

The sun has barely risen.

Tage and Alec are stretched out on each side of me, sleeping soundlessly. I wonder what time they finally came to bed?

It is still totally strange, utterly surreal, and implausibly astonishing that I get both these men. It's also fucking stifling. Their bodies are like heat conductors. I slink off the bed and lose my jeans. Even with the air blasting, I'm still perspiring. I do my business in the bathroom, grab a bottle of water from the mini fridge — which isn't so mini — and crawl back between them in just a tank top and underwear.

"You all right?" Alec places a sleepy hand on my bare thigh.

"Fine, actually." I snuggle up to him. Surprisingly, I feel much better than I thought I was going to. I only have a mild hangover, and it feels like a weight has been lifted off me. Maybe confronting Gunner was more therapeutic than I realized. It felt fucking amazing to yell at him. To scream the questions that have plagued me for years, even if I didn't get definitive answers. The scared, hurt, sixteen-year-old girl didn't have the nerve to stand up to him then, but the twenty-four-year-old woman sure did.

"Good."

"What time did you come to bed?" I whisper.

"Very late," Tage groans.

"I'll let you sleep." I kiss his tattooed shoulder.

"I'd rather fuck," he shoots back point blankly.

"I second that," Alec jumps right in.

"Nothing is stopping the two of you," I tease.

Two pairs of light-colored eyes pop open. Oh, shit, I did it now.

"Not that Alec is bad-looking, but he's a little too masculine for me." Tage pushes himself up and crawls on top of me like a predator. "You, on the other hand, are the perfect mix of sweet, soft, and feminine." He massages my breast as he covers his mouth with mine. I melt right there beneath him. I'm such a goner. Goner for both these men.

I succumb instantly, lifting my arms at his command as he drags my tank top off. Soon, I'm naked and being ravished by two hungry mouths and twenty skillful fingers. Pinching and prodding, they touch me in all the right places. I'm a sacrifice laid out on a beautifully profane altar. I drown in a deep abyss as they take turns sucking my nipples and licking my clit. My body is their wonderland. Their Zion.

Their mouths and hands my Utopia.

Moaning loudly and freely, I undulate on the bed as I'm pelted with sensations from all directions. Keeping a constant pressure of excitement, they know just how far to push me before I stumble over the edge. They have gotten way too good at working together in such a short amount of time.

"I want to watch you come." Tage nips at my ear as he plucks at my sharpened nipples. "I want to watch you ride Alec, and then I want to fuck you."

In a lusty haze, I look up at him. I would do whatever he wants. Whatever he asks. Whatever either of them asks.

Alec seems to be right on board as he repositions us on the bed. I'm so wet and aroused, I slide down onto his cock with no hindrance at all. In this position, he's buried so deep I can feel him everywhere. A fantasia of fullness flooding my reality.

"Move," Tage encourages me, lying right beside Alec. This is all brand new. They have only ever shared me, never taken turns, but the fresh dynamic is hot, erotic, and a lotta bit filthy.

I feed right into it. I want to turn them on. I want to give them everything they want.

I ride Alec commandingly, providing Tage the show he's after. It doesn't take much to put on an act. I am as much invested in this as they are. I share eye contact with one, then the other as my pleasure point rises. The feel of Alec's throbbing erection stretching me, massaging me, stabbing me in the perfect spot has me impaling his cock harder and harder. Tage said he wanted to watch me come, and he is going to get exactly that. All three of us are breathing heavy for our own reasons as my climax accelerates hard and fast.

"I'm going to come," I mewl out loud, my nipples pinching from the extreme stress my body is under. "Oh, fuck . . . oh, oh, fuck." I squeeze my eyes shut as my pussy aches, and everything inside me free falls into oblivion. All my fulfillment, all my satisfaction, all fiendish desire pours right down over Alec.

I ride him until there's nothing left. Nothing left of me, and nothing left of him.

I'm in an orgasmic-induced trance as Tage takes his turn.

Forcing me onto my back, he spreads my legs and drives himself into my soaked, sensitive pussy. The impact shocks me back to reality like an electric current.

"Ah!" I crunch up and cry as Tage begins to fuck me. He's sliding in so fast and so deep my body responds without any warning. He feels just as good as Alec, just as mind-blowing and barbaric as both these men can be.

"Tage, Tage, Tage," I pant his name with each unforgiving thrust. I'm going to come. I'm going to come, again, with both men watching me.

Tage's eyes are as wild as his hips. The sound of slapping echoes around the room, along with tense grunts and gasps for air.

My body gives out when it all becomes too much.

I splinter under Tage's bodily command, shuddering fitfully. I was given no choice. No matter how tired or spent or used I felt, he mandated the outcome.

My pelvic muscles are sore from intense constriction, my thighs are soaked from constant surges of arousal, and my head is light from extreme physical exertion.

I barely register the roar that escapes Tage's mouth or the single violent thrust that has him erupting inside me. I just know I'm a woman who belongs to two virile men.

Men who make no apologies for turning me inside out, lifting me upside down, taking what they want, and leaving me to crave so much more.

I lie lifeless on the mattress, crushed by a lofty, energy-sucking weight. Tage and Alec both lay next to me, one on each respective side, and both fucking smug as hell. They know exactly what they do to me, and it pumps up their already-inflated egos. I'm surprised there's room for all three of us on this bed.

I don't add fuel to the fire. I just lie there and bask quietly in bliss.

"Your face is red." Alec traces circles across my cheek.

"Well, you two just banged the hell out of me. What do you expect?"

Both Tage and Alec burst with laughter.

"How about we make the other set of cheeks match for that smart comment?" Tage flips me over and spanks my ass. I scream and laugh, trying to crawl away.

Tage and Alec pull me back. "Two against one. Those are totally unfair odds." I squirm beneath them as they take turns spanking me.

They both leer at me devilishly. "Oh, baby, we know."

26

T age

By MID-MORNING, I'm pulling Everly out of bed. "Time to go home, love."

"I don't want to go." She throws the covers over her head. "I just want to hide right here for the rest of my life."

"As much as you permanently fixed to a bed sounds appealing, it isn't practical. And Chicago isn't your home."

"No, never," she whines. I love it when she does that. It's cute as all hell. "But what's going to happen when we get back to New York?"

I pull the covers away from her face. "I don't know, but we'll figure it out."

"That doesn't sound promising," she pouts.

I sigh, sitting down on the mattress. "You wanna hear something that sounds promising?" She nods, her dark bangs falling into her eyes. "I promise I will never let anything bad happen to you. I promise I will never let your mother ruin the new life you worked so hard to build. I promise neither you nor Alec will feel the effects or fallout from her bad decisions. So, no matter what happens when we get back to New York, your life won't get interrupted."

"That does sound promising."

"I aim to please."

"Is it realistic, though?" Her pessimism surfaces.

"Of course, it is. If there's one thing I'm good at, it's cock-blocking. Just ask Alec."

"Tage." She hits me playfully.

"I heard that," Alec calls from the bathroom.

"It's all in the past," I shoot back, never taking my eyes off Ever.

She looks up at me lovingly, and all kinds of weird sensations grind like gears in my stomach. I have ached for her to look at me like that. To see me the way she once had. I abruptly lean down to kiss her. It's compulsive. We share an emotive moment, a gripping, profound embrace that elevates our bond to another level.

Ever inhales serenely once I pull away. "I'm glad you're here. Back with me."

"Me, too, baby." I swipe my thumb across her pink cheek. "Me, too." Being back with her is what I've wanted for a long time. "Now, come on, get up. It's time to go home. You have to go back to work tomorrow."

"I'm calling out again. Can't we spend one more day holed up in here?" Ever appeals, throwing the covers back over her head.

"I'm cool with it." Alec walks out of the bathroom towel drying his hair. It's sticking up all over the place once he's done.

"That won't look strange? Both of you taking off on the same days?" I ask him.

"Who cares?" Ever grumbles from under the covers.

"I doubt it. No one is on to us as far as I can tell. There are so many office romances flying around that place." He waves it off. "I think the policy is in place just for insurance purposes. In case something goes south. Hell, one of the senior partners is having an affair with the head of PR."

Ever throws the covers off her. "Seriously?"

"Yup," Alec confirms. "You'd be shocked from all the swapped spit in that firm."

"Have you swapped spit with anyone else?" Oh, shit. Ever just put Alec under the gun. I can't wait to hear this. I wish I had some popcorn.

"Um," he looks uncomfortable. Is it wrong I'm enjoying this so much?

"Alec?" she presses him.

"There was an intern at the Christmas party last year," he confesses. "It was just one, drunk, stupid night." He clears his throat.

She isn't amused.

"We all have a past," I remind her. There's no need to hold Alec over the fire.

Listen to me, being all mature and shit.

"True." She goes back to hiding under the covers.

Alec and I exchange a look. *What are we going to do with this girl?*

"Since we are going to spend one more night, why don't Tage and I go get some more coffee, and you take a shower? We can head down to the Riverwalk for lunch, and then hole up in here for dinner. How does that sound?" Alec peeks under the edge of the comforter.

"Caffeine?" Everly chirps. He knows just how to get to her. She spies him with one, interested eye.

"Extra large, extra sweet. I'm sure there is a fantastic coffee shop close."

"I'm in."

That didn't take much. I make a note for the future. Bribe Everly with caffeine.

"Good. Get all pretty for us while we're gone."

"I can do that," she flirts.

"I know." Alec leans down to kiss her, and she sits up, meeting him halfway. I know this should be weird, watching your girlfriend kiss another man, but strangely, it's not. It's normal. Our normal. Everly is happy with both of us, and I'm not going to be the one who rocks the boat. I'm in it for as long as she is. As long as fate will allow.

Leaving Everly to her own devices, Alec and I ride the elevator down to the lobby. We have come to coexist on a strange new level. A mutual respect has formed, and a common interest threads us together. We're direly opposite, that's for sure, but he's no bum. He's no pushover, and he's no pussy. I don't exactly know how this relationship is going to work moving forward. I'm going to need to change a lot of things in my life. Putting down roots, for starters. Working for Endeavor has me living a nomadic life, running off to all parts of the world at a moment's notice when activated. Sometimes those missions can last months at a time.

I have to find a common ground. I know there are operatives who do it. Who have a personal life and a dangerous professional one. My handler in New York is a prime example. CJ is married, has a child, and still manages to be the solid contact I need him to be. Maybe that's the route I should take? Transfer roles from field operative to handler? I'd still be part of the action, just not as much and from a much safer distance. I decide to speak to CJ when we get back to New York. It'll be easy to set up a face to face in the city.

"Hey, man. Thanks for that back there." Alec watches the floors tick down.

"For what?" My internal thought process dissolves.

"For helping me out with Everly. That would have sucked if she went all jealous girlfriend."

"No problem. Gotta have each other's back to keep the peace, right?" I respond lightly.

Alec glances over at me and smirks. "Yeah, we do."

I hold up my fist for a bump. Alec doesn't leave me hanging.

And just like that, another layer is added to our unusual and complicated relationship.

We follow the directions on Alec's GPS to the fancy schmancy coffee shop he found. He says Ever will flip over their crème brûlée latte.

To me, coffee is coffee. But if I'm honest, I like that he knows what she likes and goes out of his way to make her happy. Everly deserves happy above everything else.

The warm Chicago air is comfortable with a slight breeze coming off the water as we walk back to the hotel. I'm glad Alec talked Everly into leaving the hotel room. I think the nice day and lively atmosphere will do her some good.

As we wait for the elevator, my phone rings. I check the screen, and it's a private number. I answer immediately.

"Hello?"

"I ran through those financials you asked about," Simon gets right down to business. No hello, no good morning. He's not the social type. But he is a brilliant hacker, so his lack of manners is overlooked. By everyone. He's the star of Endeavor, really. The heart. If you need info, you go straight to him.

"And?" I sip my coffee nonchalantly as we enter the elevator.

"Nothing. No unusual activity or payments. The accounts have been dead for years."

"Fuck, okay." Dead end on Gunner's financial activity front.

"I did find one thing that was interesting, though."

"And what's that?"

"An account in the name Destiny Star Reynolds. Still active and paid up to date."

I freeze. "An account in Everly's name? What kind?" Alec spins his head in my direction, full attention, one hundred percent.

"A safe deposit box, it looks like. But the bank is strange. From what I can gather, it's new age. All digital. Facial recognition, iris scan, or fingerprint ID."

"Did you say fingerprint ID?" I look pointedly at Alec.

"I did. Would you like me to repeat it slower?"

I roll my eyes. Nothing worse than a nerdy, smartass. "No, thanks. I got it the first time." The elevator doors ding, and Alec and I step out, hanging on every word Simon is spoon-feeding us. "Where's the bank?"

"You're never gonna believe it. Chicago." He's smug.

Well, hot damn.

"Okay, thanks. Send me all the details. We'll investigate." I hang up.

"Everly is worth as much as a single fingerprint," I paraphrase Gunner's words. "I think that's it. Whatever Vicki is after is in a safe deposit box, and Everly is the only one who can access it. *She's the key.*"

Alec's face falls. "Maybe it wasn't such a good idea to leave her alone."

Unwarranted, we both barrel into the hotel room, calling Ever's name. There's no answer. We both share the same, irrational fear.

"*Ever!*" I rush into the bedroom and then the adjoining bathroom. "Ever—" I stop short, finding her in the tub, filled with bubbles, eyes closed, listening to her airpods. She has no clue I'm standing there as her head bops away to the blaring music.

I sag with relief, my heart freefalling into my stomach. A second later Alec crashes into me, finding exactly what I have. A happy, clueless Ever. I hear his audible sigh from behind me.

"Fucking-A, I nearly had a coronary."

I snicker. *Same, brother.*

Everly opens her eyes, suddenly sensing we're there. She smiles coyly, pulling out an earphone. "How long have you two Peeping Toms been there?"

"Long enough," I confirm. Picking up a towel, I lay it on the edge of the whirlpool tub. "Get out. We need to talk, love."

Everly reads the grim tone of my voice. This conversation is going to be so much fucking fun.

Alec and I watch like the Peeping Toms we are as Everly stands, gloriously wet and naked, and washes herself off. I will never tire of seeing her bare body. I think both Alec and I are salivating from just watching the innocent, sexy show.

Once Ever is dry and wrapped in a plushy, white hotel robe, we sit her down on the couch and hand her the coffee. Alec and I silently agree that making her as comfortable as possible will lessen the blow.

"What is going on with you two?" She holds her crème brûlée coffee with both hands and regards us strangely.

Alec looks to me to take the lead. "Ever." I search for the right words to begin. "I think we figured out why Gunner locked you away all those years ago and what your mom is after now."

Her pretty green eyes widen threefold.

"The key your mom is after isn't a traditional key. It's you. You're the key."

"Huh?"

Rightfully, she's confused. I scoot closer to her on the couch. "It looks like Gunner opened a safe deposit box in your name. And your fingerprint is the only way to access it. Whatever's inside must be worth something substantial."

"Like three years of my life," she comments bitterly.

"That, and maybe much more."

"How much more can he possibly take?" she snaps. Her anger is warranted. What Gunner did was monumentally wrong. What her mother did was worse because she allowed it. "You know what? I don't care what's in that box. I don't care about Gunner or my mother. Let her come after me. Let her try and force my hand. I'm not scared of her. She won't intimidate me. I won't let her." Ever shoots to her feet. "Alec, give me your phone."

Alec stares up at her, confused. "For what?"

"I need to call my mother."

"Ever," I interject.

"Tage," she bites. She isn't having it. "I'm going to tell her to fuck off once and for all."

"As much as I admire your tenacity right now" — Alec reaches for her — "I don't think telling her off is going to do much."

"It will make me feel a hell of a lot better. Phone. Now."

Alec flat out refuses. "You're poking the snake with the stick."

"I don't care," she huffs.

Alec looks at me. I shake my head no.

"Dammit, you two." Ever stomps her foot. "I have to stand up for myself at some point. I'm tired of hiding in a hole. I'm tired of her thinking she can do what she wants to me. That she can threaten me and the people I love. Alec, give me the fucking phone."

The room is soberingly quiet. The last thing I want is Everly contacting her mother in any way, shape, or form. But on the flip side, I wonder if Vicki will back off with a threat from her daughter.

"Give it to her," I direct Alec. "Let's see what happens."

"Tage," Alec argues.

"Do it." I push.

Begrudgingly, Alec hands over the phone.

"It's locked," Everly gripes.

Nice try, Alec.

Alec presses his thumb on the circle, unlocking what may be the worst decision the three of us have ever made.

Everly squints as she scrolls through Alec's calls. She can't see well without her glasses, but she manages to find what she's looking for. Heaven help us all.

She stomps into the center of the room with Alec and I hawking her every move. Everly paces the bright, sunny space as the phone rings.

Then she pauses, and my heart ceases to beat.

"Mom," she growls, and not like the adorable puppy she is, like a fierce wolf about to rip someone's throat out. "Listen carefully, 'cause I'm only going to say this once. Leave me the fuck alone. I'll never give you what's in that box out of spite alone. I would cut off all my fingers and feed them to a dog before I let you have it. Stop stalking me, stop threatening Alec, and fucking drop dead." She hangs up and chucks the phone back at Alec. He has good reflexes thankfully, if not, he would have ended up with a black eye.

Everly is heaving by the time it's all said and done. I'm unsure what to do next. Should I get up and hug her, or pour her a strong drink?

"Ever, you okay?" I ask delicately.

She looks over at me and Alec still seated on the couch. I have never seen that look in her eyes before. It is beyond ferocious.

"No, Tage. I am not fucking okay." Her words are eerily calm.

Then she's walking. Alec and I both stand. "Where are you going?" He follows her, as concerned as me.

"Back into the tub, to drown myself." Her statement is more face-tious than anything, but still underlying alarming.

Alec and I stalk Everly into the bathroom. She already has the water running and her robe dropped. Stepping into the nearly empty tub, she sits down, curls herself into a ball, and cries.

Christ, this girl and everything she's been through.

"Ever." Alec kicks his shoes off, then loses his clothes. "Baby, it's okay." He draws her against his naked body and lets her unload all her emotions into his neck. He looks up at me as I stand there like a dufus. I'm not good at all this crying stuff. He jerks his head, communicating to me to get my ass in the tub. He doesn't have to tell me twice.

I strip down and climb into the tub, Alec repositioning him and Everly, so I can snuggle up to her free side.

As much of a cocky bastard as he is, Alec is much better in the emotions department than I am. He seems to handle outbursts and crying like a pro. At the moment, I'm thankful for that.

"That was pretty badass," Alec hums to Ever. "You had me scared."

Everly laughs through her tears. "Alec, shut up."

"I'm being serious. I know who I'm sending next time I have to squeeze a client."

"Yeah, my glasses and braids are really going to intimidate them." She wipes her face. The water is nearly covering her chest now.

"That's the angle. They'll never expect such an innocent-looking badass. We'll call you Ghostface Killer."

She scoffs at the name.

"I know a place that can fill that job description," I chime in.

In no time, Alec and I have Everly smiling more than frowning. We don't make a half-bad team.

Once the water reaches max capacity, I turn the faucet off, and the three of us just sit and soak in the steaming hot water. We'll spend all day in here if that's what it'll take to make Ever happy.

"It felt good." Ever vacantly places her palm on the surface of the clear water. "Telling her off."

"She definitely deserved it," I agree.

"Think she'll back off?" Everly slides her eyes up to meet mine.

I shake my head solemnly. My gut tells me no.

"Yeah, me neither."

"We'll figure it out." I caress her thigh.

"Maybe I should go back into hiding? If I'm out of the picture, no one can get hurt."

"Ever, no," Alec protests immediately.

"She won't be able to get what she wants. And Alec, your career won't be in danger," Everly argues.

I stay silent. In my professional opinion, it's not the worst idea. Everly and I could easily disappear, but where would that leave Alec? Could he just drop everything — his high-powered career, his friends, his family — and up and vanish? That is a hard ship to sail away on.

It's easier for me since I'm a ghost. I have no attachments, no family or core set of friends. I've been a loner since the age of sixteen. I can disappear and no one would come looking.

"I don't think my career is in danger. I think your mom is bluffing, honestly. If she was going to pull something, it would have happened by now. She would have greased the wheels, but it's been three days and nothing."

"The possibility, though." Everly doesn't seem on board with Alec's argument. I tend to agree with him. By now, if Vicki had the means, she would have pulled something.

"Well, if I can't disappear" — Everly pokes holes in the surface of the water — "maybe we should find out what's in that box."

"Seriously?" I sit up.

"Why not? If we get rid of the contents, we get rid of the problem."

"Umm . . ." Alec disagrees. "I'm not sure it works like that."

"Me neither."

"What other option do we have besides having my mother killed?"

"You can be scary. Maybe we should start calling you Ghostface Killer?" I comment, proud as hell of the woman she's become.

"I'm just saying." Ever laughs. "I want her gone once and for all. Please, Tage." She rubs up against me and purrs.

"You want me to kill your mother?" Not that I wouldn't.

"No." She splashes me. "I want you to take me to see what's in that box. And if getting rid of it doesn't work, *then* I want you to kill her." There's that evil sarcasm again.

"I'll represent you during your murder trial," Alec adds flippantly.

Well, gee, thanks.

"Pro bono," Everly stipulates.

"Of course." Alec snorts.

"I'm glad you two are having so much fun at my expense." And I thought I could be ruthless.

"It's easy to do." Everly giggles. She is so lucky she's cute. "So, what do you say?" She floats into Alec's welcoming arms. He is clearly on board with this plan.

"Fine," I relent. "We'll go see what's in the box. But we need to case the place first. I don't want us walking in blind."

"I'm excellent at research," Alec boasts.

"A high-powered lawyer, I'd hope so," I mock.

"It's decided, then." Everly stands up dripping wet. Alec and I pant like dogs. "We go see what's in the box."

"Where are you going?" I grab at her leg as she steps over me.

"Well, I was hoping the two of you could take care of *my* box before we tend to the other box."

Alec and I stand up faster than an Olympic sprinter at the sound of the gun. All Everly has to do is hint she wants us and we are ready and willing.

The three of us are still wet from the tub, but that doesn't stop the momentum. Alec and I manhandle Everly into the position we want. Situated on all fours, Alec settles behind her with me kneeling in front of her.

"Alec's gonna come in that sweet pussy of yours, while I come in your hot little mouth." I quake with lust.

Alec and I make eye contact. He nods and so do I. This is about taking care of so much more than Everly's box.

I caress her face, coaxing her to open her mouth. Just as she does, Alec sinks inside of her. Her moan around my cock is insatiable. It's greedy and ravenous. She loves to get taken, to be ruled, to be commanded.

Alec fucks her slow, as I indulge in the back and forth motion of her body, her mouth sliding over my erection, making it slick with saliva and pulsing with pleasure.

It's a prolonged build to her climax. A drawn-out dance that has us wringing the ecstasy from her little by little.

Trapped between us, she has no choice but to submit, to succumb to our speed. Alec drives deep into her pussy at the same exact time I thrust animalistically into her mouth. A carnal union of arousal has us ensnared. The three of us shaken, stirred, and stimulated all at the same time. Hot breaths, sexual noises, and guttural strains play out like a concentrated harmony all around the room. It's a frenzy of push and pull, jostle and jerk as Alec and I propel Everly straight to her breaking point.

She's beautiful to fucking watch. A woman so strong and smart, breaking down under our control. The craving, the longing, the yearning. The lust and passion. The ache and throb. It all comes together in a vortex of voracity.

"Aw, shit, baby, you want more?" Alec grunts, the thrusts of his pelvis becoming more erratic. "You need to come?" He concentrates hard as Ever begins to push back and suck harder.

She whines so desperately, inhaling air fanatically through her nose.

I barely have to move, the force of Alec's hips and the clamp of Ever's mouth have me in the perfect position. I dig my fingers into her hair and grip the thick strands tightly, keeping my body stiff. I watch Alec fuck her, getting off on every stoke and every moan he elicits.

Everly's arms give way when she finally comes, the pressure of her mouth and pull of her lips around my erection has me seeing stars. I pump my hips greedily, grunting wildly until I follow her right down the same orgasmic rabbit hole. My whole being gravitates toward her mouth as Alec rings out every drop of her pleasure. It's a domino effect and a three-way connection all rolled up into one ravenousness moment.

I'm left shaking on my knees, my cock still firmly secure in Ever's mouth, her small, spacy sucks sending aftershocks to my balls.

"Fuck, baby, I love you, and that hot mouth." I groan, supremely satisfied. I told you, I'm not great with the lovey-dovey stuff, but I'm working on it.

"I love you, too," she emotes after she pops my semi from between her lips and stands up on her knees. She leans back against Alec for support as we share a heated, dizzying kiss. She then does the same with him.

Stunning, adventurous, majestic, I could call Everly Paige a thousand things, but my favorite thing to call her, by far, is *ours*.

27

E verly

Tage and Alec spend a majority of the day researching the Dominus Savings and Trust while I stare at my fingertip. The small, seemingly insignificant part of my body is what Gunner wanted all along. Not me, just the print of my little finger.

I try to think back all those years ago to a time, an instance, where he could have fingerprinted me. Did he lift it from a door knob? A fork? A glass? How does this whole thing work? Questions upon questions upon questions mount.

"Okay." Alec pushes himself back from Tage's laptop. "From what I can gather this 'bank' is totally unique and state of the art. It's accessible twenty-four-seven with a facial rec, retina scan, or finger-print ID."

"So, we can just stroll in at midnight?" I snort.

"Yup," Tage smacks his lips, "and that's exactly what we're going to do. Providing your print can really get us into the building."

"Why midnight?" I question him.

"Safer. No one out and about. Hide under the cover of night. You know, all that spy stuff." He winks.

"Sounds mysterious," I poke fun.

"You may think it's funny, but protocol is there for a reason, and it keeps you alive." Most of the time.

"I don't think protocol is funny. I think the way you aloofly described it is."

"Fair enough. Here's the deal. I'll have some Endeavor eyes watching us while we go in. We'll check it out, see what the goods are, and then we'll get the hell out. After that, the agency can decide what to do. I'm hoping there isn't anything radioactive, 'cause that would surely suck."

"Radioactive?" Alec curls his lip.

Tage shrugs. "He's a criminal. I wouldn't put anything past him."

"Do you think we should rent hazmat suits?" I toss in.

"Nah, as long as it's contained, we should be fine."

No one is laughing.

It's MIDNIGHT, and we are standing outside a polished-looking building in the middle of Chicago's financial district.

"Moment of truth." Tage pushes me forward. My stomach flip-flops. I'm torn down the middle. I desperately want to know what Gunner locked away, and I desperately don't.

"Fingerprint scan." Alec points out a little square with reddish glass next to one of the doors.

Moment of truth. I take a deep breath with each one of them by my side and press my index finger to the glass.

We wait. Nothing.

"Huh?" I try again, but nothing happens.

"Try your thumb," Tage suggests.

I press my thumb to the glass with little faith, and the door clicks. "Holy shit."

"We're in." Tage yanks open the steel door, and it creaks.

Inside the building is all bright fluorescent lights, creamy floors, ceilings, and walls. "Okay" — Tage reads his phone — "according to Simon, we need to take the elevator to the sixth floor. That's where the safe deposit box is."

"Let's not waste a second, then." Alec walks, and we follow. The elevators are only a little way down the hall. Again, I have to use my thumbprint to access them. Once inside, we hit the number six.

Holy. Shit. This is really happening.

The elevator ride is smooth, and we arrive to our desired floor in no time. When the door separates, we are met by all white and a wall of frosted glass.

"Whoa." All three of us step up to a clear door. Inside there are dozens upon dozens of safes. It looks like a lockbox mausoleum.

Tage knocks on the glass lightly. "I think this is bulletproof."

"I hope so because that'd be mighty tempting for a thief," Alec observes.

"Let's get this over with." I'm antsy all of a sudden. My invisibility high from earlier seems to be wearing off quick.

I press my thumb to the door scan, and like with the elevators and steel door earlier, it clicks. We open it and step inside.

There has to be two-hundred safe deposit boxes set in the walls. All in one little room.

"We need to find number nineteen-ninety-one." Tage begins reading each box. It takes a minute, but we finally find what we're looking for.

"Number nineteen-ninety-one," Alec reads aloud. "Do your thing."

"Do my thing, right." Like I'm a fucking magician or something. Taking another deep breath, I press my thumb to the scanner on the face of the box door. It takes an elongated second, but it does, in fact, open.

"Holy-fucking-shit." Tage's eyes are big as shiny satellites. It's like a chapter of the past is finally closing. A journey we could have only taken together.

Alec pulls the shiny silver box out and places it on the white glossy table in the middle of the room. The three of us stand before it, mesmerized as to what can possibly be inside.

Alec flips the clasp and opens the lid. We all stare down inside.

"What in the flying fuck?" Tage barks as he inspects the contents.

Butterflies erupt in my stomach as sweet reminders from my past gaze up at me.

"Hello Kitty." I grab one of the adorable, plastic bobble heads from the box. "I used to love these." I shake the toy, and her kitty head dances.

"This is what Gunner hid away? This is what your mother is after? A bunch of kiddy toys?" It's anticlimactic, to say the least.

I shrug. "The one stinkin' good memory I have of Gunner is him giving me these. He always had one for me when he and my mom started dating. The best part about them," I twist the base, and it detaches from the body. "There was always candy inside."

I hold up the secret tube.

"I don't think that's candy." Alec's jaw nearly unhinges.

"Not at all." Tage takes the bottom part of the toy from my hand and holds it up to the fluorescent light. The tiny, clear gems in the tube sparkle with colorful prisms.

"Are those . . . *diamonds?*" They must be, because my lady bits are totally tingling.

"Holy motherfucking shit." Tage reiterates. "Gunner and his goddamn riddles. Even if someone else opened this box, only you knew the real secret."

"Gotta have some respect for the evil mastermind. That is sort of genius." Alec crosses his arms, impressed.

"All those months I worked undercover. I knew about the drugs and the guns, but never this. No one had any idea Gunner was running diamonds, too."

"My mom did." I'm so disappointed. So disappointed in the woman who birthed me. Who was supposed to protect me. Raise me. *Love me.*

"She definitely knew something." Tage is totally spellbound by the glinty little stones.

"Seven, eight, nine, ten," Alec counts all the Hello Kitty dolls. "Thirteen, fourteen, fifteen. Fifteen dolls all stuffed with diamonds. There has to be close to ten-million dollars here, easy."

"Ten-million reasons for my mom to come after me." And there it is. What she wanted the whole time. A new pipeline for her fix.

Tage pulls his phone out of his back pocket as we congregate around the table.

"Andrews." He turns his back to us. "What? . . . When? . . . *How?* . . . That is a maximum-security prison."

My eyes fly to the back of his head.

"What's your ETA? . . . Okay . . . Okay." Click. Tage spins. "We need to go. Now." He morphs into super-spy mode.

"What happened?" I ask, alarmed, as Tage puts all the contents back in the box, closes it up, and slides it back into the wall in record time.

"Very bad shit." He grabs my arm. Hard — *ouch* — and yanks me out of the bank.

"What kind of very bad shit?" Alec presses, hot on our heels.

Tage doesn't respond. He's too busy using my finger like a hot poker to hit the elevator button, crazier than a madman.

When the elevator doors finally open, we are met by the barrel of a gun and three very unwelcome faces.

"That kind of bad shit." Tage curses.

I almost can't believe what I'm seeing. A tattooed goon, my mother, *and Gunner*, all together, all playing nice. *What the fuck is happening here?*

"Hi, sweetheart." My mom steps out of the elevator first. I barely recognize her. She actually looks good. Fresh-faced, nice clothes, neat hair. I'm at a loss for words for the woman standing before me. The woman I share no traits with except DNA.

Gunner and the goon with the gun follow her.

"In," Gunner orders.

Oh, fuck.

Tage never lets go of my arm as we're marched back into the bank. When the glass door clicks closed, my throat constricts. *This is so bad. So. Fucking. Bad.*

"You were a total let-down," my mother disses Alec.

"Why? 'Cause I didn't crumble to pieces when you threatened me?"

"Yes. I totally read you wrong. I never thought my daughter would be more important to you than your career."

"You've never been the best judge of character," I mouth off. "Case in point," I refer to Gunner and his goon.

"I missed you, too, sweetheart," she sneers.

"I didn't miss you. At all. And I have never been your sweetheart."

"I never coddled you. You always resented me." The brown-haired bitch is right, I have always resented her. But not because she didn't coddle me. Because she never wanted me.

"Total bullshit. You never cared. That's what I resented."

"Enough," Gunner grumbles. "Open it already. We need to get out of here."

"I'm not opening shit." I clench my fists.

"Oh, no?" Gunner nods, and the guy with the gun points it at Alec's head. I visibly tremble. "We make this simple or hard, pretty. Open the safe, no one gets hurt. Fight me, he goes first, then him." He looks at Tage. "Then you."

"What did you say about cutting off your fingers?" my mother asks condescendingly. "We can totally do that."

"You're full of shit." Tage pulls me closer. "None of us are walking out of here alive once you get what you want."

"I guess that's a gamble you are going to have to take, groundhog."

"Gamble on your words? No, thanks," Tage hisses.

"How come you didn't just die the first time?" Gunner groans.

"You're a shitty shot?" Tage offers superciliously.

"Let's see." Gunner pulls out a gun from the back of his waistband and points it right at Tage.

I don't know what suddenly comes over me, a moment of insanity, maybe? A suicidal mindset perhaps— death-or-glory, do-or-die?

"No!" I scream, pushing Gunner's arm away. It goes off, and instantly all hell breaks loose.

Tage dives at Gunner, wrestling him to the floor. Gunner's hit man points and shoots, and then Alec is in front of me. Then, he's not. He's on the ground. Bleeding.

"*Alec!*" I screech one octave lower than a dog can hear. Everyone in the room grinds to a halt.

"*Alec!*" I try to reach for him, but I'm grabbed. "*Alec,*" I fight, "*Alec . . .*" I'm having déjà vu.

"*Save him!*" *I scream as they tear me away.* "*You have to save him!*" *I flail in the stranger's arms in a fit of panic, reaching for the window.*

Gunner drags me out of the room with a gun to my head. Tage looks like he wants to bolt after us but is stuck to the floor.

"Move, and she's fucking dead."

The glass door swings closed, and the elevator doors ding open. The last vision I see is Tage frozen, and Alec bleeding out on the floor.

Alec . . .

The elevator ride is hazy. I'm in shock, back in the hands of the two people I hate the most. *How did this happen?*

"Did the two of you have it all planned?" I ask, removed. "To ruin my life again?"

"We just wanted what was ours." My mother's answer is foul. It's like she can barely stand to converse with me.

"How did you break out of jail?" I look up at Gunner through blurry eyes.

"Lots of money, the right contacts, and a stellar escape plan. The only thing I didn't bank on was your boyfriend still being in the picture. All my intel told me he was history. And then you fucking showed up with him. How did you know?"

"Tage was never out of the picture. He's just a master at disguising himself." I'm smug. I'm about to lose everything, might as well try and hold on to my attitude. "I remembered you two fighting about a key. We researched. It wasn't hard. You're not that smart."

"Aren't I?" The ugly, faded tattoos on his neck dance as he looks down at me. "I have you. You're the only one who can open that box. My fingerprint may work on the door and elevator, but that box and those contents belong solely to you."

We walk down the light hallways to the steel door we entered through as Gunner verbally vomits. I don't care about a thing he's saying. I don't care about what he's going to do to me or what he fucking wants. All I care about is Alec.

Please God, let him live. Let him be okay.

"And there are a lot of people I owe. I need those diamonds. This isn't over."

We bust through the door and are met by cop cars, flashing lights, and a dozen automatic weapons. My heart nearly gives out from the surprise.

"Put your weapon on the ground and back away from the hostage," someone yells, but the four of us are deer in headlights.

Gunner snakes his arm around my neck and chokes me, pressing the barrel of his gun to my temple.

"I'll kill her, I swear." He walks down the sidewalk with my mother and his goon safely behind him.

"Gunner, let the girl go. There's no way out," the same deep, rumbly voice continues to address him.

Gunner laughs. The sound is as evil as a demon. "There's always a way out."

The seconds pound away like a gong as imminent death surrounds me. One wrong move. One wrong decision, and I am dead.

"Gunner," the man warns as he keeps walking. I silently pray, not for myself, but for Alec and Tage. For Lara and Luke. For all the people I love. I pray a silent thank you for the brief happiness I was allowed to have. For the friends I was blessed with. I pray for their lives and their joy. It's all I can give. My prayers are all I've ever really had.

There's a strange clicking sound before Gunner spontaneously pushes me to the ground and opens fire. I curl into a terrified ball as the bullets fly over my head. Then there's a huge cloud of smoke choking me. I keep my eyes closed until the madness ends, covering my ears from the loud torrents of cracking bursts.

Terrified tears stream down my face, and then there's suddenly nothing. No sound, no smoke. No Gunner.

It's only a split second before a man is scooping me off the ground.

"It's okay, you're safe now. I've got you." Shaking, I wrap my arms around his neck and look up into a pair of warm, unfamiliar, brown eyes. He isn't dressed like a policeman. Instead, he's wearing black fatigues.

"Alec, Tage." I come to my senses as the man carries me to a blacked-out SUV. "Alec, he's shot."

"We know. There's a team going up to get him now." Red and blue lights flash, nearly blinding me. It looks like a war zone with all the emergency personnel scattered around.

"Who're you?" I ask, beside myself.

"CJ." He smiles brightly. "I work with Tage." He winks.

"Oh, you're one of *them*."

"I am," he confirms. "But shhh, I was never here, and you never met me." I think CJ is trying to be funny, maybe trying to take the edge off, but my sense of humor is currently absent.

"Where's Gunner?" My panic though, is most definitely present.

"Gone. He got away. He's a slick one." CJ scowls. He has the same kind of authoritative air as Tage. A blue-coat kind of persona.

"Gone?" My throat closes, but I don't have time to dwell as Alec is rolled out on a stretcher.

"Alec." I scoot out of the backseat and book it toward him. Tage is with him. His hands are bloody, and so is his white shirt.

"Alec, Alec." I try to fight the tears. He doesn't respond.

"Is he going to be okay?" I turn to Tage as they lift him into the ambulance.

"I don't know," He's brutally honest.

"Do you two want to ride with?" the EMT asks right before he closes the door.

"Yes." I catapult myself into the bus.

Tage follows.

"Hey!" CJ yells. "Tage, get her checked for trauma!"

Slam. The doors close, and we speed away.

Trauma? I'm unquestionably afflicted by that.

Alec is hooked up to all kinds of tubes and has an oxygen mask on. There is so much blood. *So. Much. Blood.*

I watch the heart rate monitor obsessively as Tage cleans off his hands.

"You're going to be okay. You're going to get through this," I pray. I pray so fucking hard. Alec doesn't deserve this. He doesn't deserve to lose his life. *This is my fault. This is all my fault.* "Alec, please. Fight." Tears stream down my face like an angry river.

"He's strong. He'll fight." Tage holds me close.

The ambulance ride is bumpy, but thankfully short. Three more silent prayers later, they are rolling him out of the back of the ambulance into the emergency room.

We can only follow him so far as doctors and nurses check his vitals and call out things completely foreign to me.

The operating room they wheel him into has a window so we can see almost everything that's happening.

That thin piece of glass is the only thing keeping me on my feet. The only thing supporting my sluggish body.

I fall slowly to pieces as the minutes tick by and the surgeons work quickly tending to Alec.

Tage stands right next to me, watching in silence everything I am. All the carnage.

I start to weep. The pressure finally taking its toll. Alec has become a permanent part of my heart. *Without him, how will I live?*

How will I survive?

Tage wraps his arm around me and kisses my head. He speaks softly to me, but I can't comprehend a word he says. I can't comprehend anything right now.

I can't comprehend how someone as amazing as Alec is currently fighting for his life. Karma is fucking cruel.

"Andrews." That same, deep timber from earlier startles me out of my internal breakdown.

"Commander Adams." Tage stands at attention and salutes the man. He's tall, broad, and imposing. Dressed exactly like CJ in those same black fatigues.

"Gunner's in the wind. We're putting together a task force. We need you to head it, son. You know him best. Know his patterns."

"Yes, sir." Tage takes a step forward, and I grab his arm.

"You can't leave." I nearly explode into a million pieces.

Both Tage and the Commander stare down at me, each for a different reason.

"Alec could die. You can't leave me alone. I need you." My plea is earnest.

This is what he promised me. That he wouldn't abandon me again. That he would be here. *Always.*

Creases around Tage's eyes appear. Oh, no. No, no, no. I know that look. I have had nightmares for years about that look.

"Don't." I shake my head insanely. "Don't do it again. *You promised.*"

With that, Commander Adams steps away, giving us some space.

"As long as he's out there, neither of us will ever have peace." Tage's response is sorrowful, but also full of vengeance.

"You promised me," I desperately repeat. I can't lose both of them. I just can't.

"You will always be the most important thing in my life." Tage traps my face and presses his lips to my forehead.

"Then fucking stay." I shove him away.

"Everly, I can't." Tage traces my cheek tenderly. The contact makes me sick because I'm certain it will be the last time. The last time I ever feel his touch, or see his face, or stand in his presence. The tears come harder and faster than they ever had before.

"Ever, don't." He kisses me, swiftly and powerfully, as if that is supposed to ease the pain. As if the pain of him leaving me could ever be taken away. I kiss him back with all the might I have, hoping upon hope the impassioned embrace will make him stay. Will change his mind, will force him to come to his senses.

I love you. I always have. I always will.

Tage... please stay.

The heart monitor in Alec's room flat lines, grabbing my attention. I break the kiss and throw myself against the glass. *No! No! No!*

"*Tage,*" I turn around hysterically, but he's gone.

I'm alone.

I'm falling apart.

And there's no one left to turn to.

28

lec

BEEEEEEEEEEEP . . .

I hear the ear-piercing ring in the distance as I look into the light. All the physical pain is gone, but my heart still hurts.

My life has not been fulfilled.

There's business still left on this Earth for me to tend to.

But the call of the light is powerful. It beckons me. Sheer peace awaits me on the other side. Of this, I'm sure. I feel it seeping through the warm beams reaching out to touch my skin.

The annoying ring is getting louder, though, cutting through the tranquility flooding my being.

"Clear."

I'm literally shocked, and the rays of light and divine serenity disappear right before my eyes.

Then there's pain. Ungodly pain.

Blip . . . blip . . . blip . . .

THE SOUND of heavy rain wakes me.

I feel strange. Heavy, but light.

It's hard to move.

I look around the foreign room. It's cream in color, with large windows and lots of machines.

Where am I?

Then I remember. The gun, Everly, Tage's bloody hands, blacking out.

I jolt from the onslaught of memories.

Then she's there. Holding my hand, smiling down at me with watery eyes.

"Hey, it's okay." Ever presses loving kisses all over my face. "Welcome back."

I find my bearings, then ask, "How long was I out?" My voice is foreign and groggy.

"Three days."

"Whoa." I clear my throat.

"Yeah. You gave us a scare." She presses a button on the wall next to my bed as she wipes her wet eyes, smiling. "I don't think I've stopped crying for one minute."

That breaks my heart.

"Babe." I pathetically pull on her hand. I'm seriously weak.

A nurse appears. "Welcome back, Mr. Prescott." She's cheery. It's annoying. The nurse checks this and that, my vitals and pulse, and records them on the clipboard. Ever watches, seemingly overcome with joy. "I'll let the doctor know you're awake. He'll be in to examine you in a few minutes. Great girl you have here. She didn't leave your side for a minute." The nurse with dark hair and fluorescent red lipstick winks at Everly.

Ever smiles in return.

Then it's just us again.

"You never left?" I ask.

"Not for one second. The firm pulled a string and got you moved into a private room with an extra bed for me." She thumbs behind her at the messy sheets.

"So, our secret is out?"

Everly nods. "I quit."

"You what? Ever," I scold her. That's the last thing she should have done. Her future was so promising at the firm.

"Alec," she silences me. "You saved me." She sounds in awe. "You stepped in front of a gun for me."

"It was the chivalrous thing to do." I shift and am stabbed in the ribs with pain. "Fuck."

"It was insane," she goes on, trying to comfort me. Fluffing my pillow, kissing my lips, pouring me a glass of water.

"It was instinctual. I just reacted." I sip slowly, the cool liquid quenching the desert-like thirst.

"It was heroic."

"Tage is the hero. He was the one who kept me calm, kept pressure on the wound, and talked me through it. You know, until I passed out." I recall the terrorizing moments. "I was freaking out. I was bleeding, they took you, there was so much happening so fast. Tage just kept reassuring me you were going to be okay. That we were both going to be okay."

"Tage definitely has vigilante tendencies." She sighs.

"Where is Riggs?" I make a *Lethal Weapon* joke. Tage definitely has the hair, the attitude, and the death wish.

"Gone." Everly breaks the news.

"Gone? Gone where? Is he coming back?"

She shakes her head solemnly. "I don't think so. Not this time."

"What?" I squeeze her hand, seeing the devastation in her eyes. I know what he meant to her. Everything they've been through. He was supposed to change. He made a promise. We both did.

"Can I be honest?" Everly clears her throat of all the emotion.

"Always."

"I never really believed he was going to stay." Her voice is a strained whisper. "It's over. We're over. We've finally said goodbye."

"And you're okay with that?" It's almost preposterous to hear. I had gotten used to our threesome so fast, it felt as if it was written in stone.

She shrugs, teary-eyed. "I have to be. If there's one thing Tage made me good at, it was saying goodbye to him."

"That's sad."

"It is," she agrees.

"So, it's just you and me, then?" I re-evaluate. The lawyer mentality is never far away.

"It's just you and me," she confirms. "If you still want me. Knowing I'm unemployed. Knowing my past. Knowing there could still be trouble in my future." She rattles off a dozen reasons for me to run. None scary enough, though. I'm not going anywhere. Not without her.

"What kind of trouble?"

"Gunner got away. He's out there, somewhere. With my mom and that crazy man with the gun."

"And Tage went after them." I fit the puzzle pieces together. Only something catastrophic could pull him away from Everly. Of this, I'm sure. Gunner being on the run definitely fits that bill.

"He said neither of us would ever find peace of mind as long as he's free."

"Is he right?" I search her beautiful face. I didn't realize how much I missed it until now.

"Maybe. But knowing Tage is out there lessens the burden. I won't stop my life. I refuse. And I won't sacrifice a future with you. That is, if you still want one with me." She bites her lip. She burns so brightly even in her moments of doubt.

I tap my chest, gesturing her to lie next to me. She's too far away.

Everly crawls into the hospital bed carefully and rests her head exactly where I patted myself on the chest.

"I don't think there is another woman in this world who deserves my brave, fearless, courageous, daredevil, dashingly handsome, one-of-a-kind-self more than you."

"Oh," she laughs. "You have a mighty high opinion of yourself."

"I took a bullet. My hubris is warranted." I'm smug.

"Hubris. That's such a cocky lawyer word."

"Last time I checked, I was a cocky lawyer." I grin.

"My favorite cocky lawyer in the whole entire world." She snuggles up against me. Nothing feels more right.

"The cocky lawyer who would take a bullet for you."

"And share his future with me," she adds.

"The cocky lawyer who would do anything for you." I tilt her chin up.

"I would do anything for you, too." She touches her lips sweetly to mine, binding the prospect of a whole new day.

A whole relationship.

A whole new existence.

A whole new future.

Just the two of us.

Her and me.

EPILOGUE

Tage
Eight months later

I KNOW, I'm an asshole.

And this time, I totally care.

I thought I could do it. Give up the life. Be with Everly. Be normal. Somewhat. But as soon as the offer was presented, my intrinsic instincts kicked in. I didn't give it a second thought. If I was really a changed man, I would have. I would have stayed.

But I'm a hunter by nature. The thrill of the chase gives me life. Maybe that's why I pursued Ever. She was always a chase. Even when we were finally together. I was always battling Alec in some way or form. There was always a push and pull, a challenge. I'm not saying it's right. I'm saying it just is. It's who I am.

I found myself in the exact same situation as eight years ago. I needed to make a choice, and I went with my gut.

History repeated itself.

Everly means the world to me, no matter the circumstance. She always will. She was my first love. I was her first everything. No one can ever take that. Our memories. Our precious moments. But she deserves better. Someone, so much better than me.

Alec is that person. He's that man. He can take care of her better than I ever could. He can hand her the world on a silver platter. He can also hand over his heart and his commitment. I've never been good at commitment, unless you count my commitment to duty. I've always been married to that.

It was my other first love.

It may be the only love I can ever hold on to.

The march winds whip in New York City, but the day is bright and clear.

I stand on the sidewalk in a baseball cap and denim jacket spying inside a storefront window. I haven't been back to New York in eight months. I have scoured the world looking for Gunner, coming so close to catching him I could almost hear the click of the handcuffs. But he's smart, and he has contacts coming out of his ass. I discovered he had his plan in motion for years. Coordinating the whole thing from the blind cover of his jail cell.

But I'm going to get him, even if it takes my entire life to do so. Like I said, I'm a hunter by nature, I live for the thrill of the chase, and I always get my man.

I watch covertly as the pretty redhead in the middle of the store smiles and laughs with a leggy blonde who's sitting on a fancy couch outlined with gold leaf, sipping champagne.

She's absolutely glowing, and it hurts my heart as much as it makes it fly high. That's all I ever wanted for her. For her to smile just like that. Carefree. Untroubled. Lighthearted. Alec is doing a good job of making her happy.

Ever is dressed in a long, beautiful wedding gown that hugs her waist, with ruffles and sparkles, and all sorts of things I can barely describe.

She's stunning, though. Every inch of her. Especially her long red hair. She dyed it back, and for the first time in a long time I see the true Everly. The mysterious being I fell head over heels in love with the moment I saw her.

My heart beat still accelerates and my pulse still pounds the exact same way it did that night. The first night I noticed her, gazing longingly through her bedroom window. Trapped. Alone. Sad. For a short time, I was her savior. And that short time I will always cherish. A sixteen-year old-girl taught me so much about myself. About who I am and who I could possibly be. She made me stronger, and she didn't even know it. I didn't know it either until I had to walk away.

I hold the pink piece of paper in my hand, shielded by the wind in my pocket. I swiped it back the morning after Alec, Everly, and I consummated our relationship. I just couldn't part with it. Maybe it was a prediction of what was to come. I didn't think I would leave her then, but I walked away so easily when offered the opportunity. Now, like before, this note is the last tangible thing I have left of her.

I'll never let go of it.

Ever.

The blonde stands up off the couch and takes Everly's empty champagne glass. She walks away, leaving Ever alone in the center of the room. She gazes dreamily at herself in the mirror. The long veil making her look like a tried-and-true bride. The most beautiful bride I have ever seen.

Alec is a lucky man.

As if spooked by something, Everly pauses, then slowly peers over her shoulder.

Anxiety smashes a hole through my chest like a sledgehammer.

I should move, hide, get the hell out of dodge, but I don't. I stand my ground. And as if she senses exactly where I am, she looks directly into my eyes.

A connection that could cross seas and scale mountains passes between us.

A split second of time is shared only by us.

Everly smiles somberly. I will ache for eternity from that expression. There's no bitterness or hatred portrayed in her eyes. Only amnesty, acquittal, absolution.

She let go.

She let go of *me*, and she forgives me.

Forgiveness is not what I came here looking for, though.

I made my choice.

I stand by it, and I'm prepared to live the rest of my life with the consequences. As heart-wrenching as they may be.

I just wanted to see her one last time.

One last time ...

One last time . . . before she officially became *his*.

The End

Thank you so much for reading A.C.H.E.! I hope you enjoyed Everly, Tage, and Alec's ride! You can check out more M. Never books at www.mneverauthor.com <3

ABOUT THE AUTHOR

M. Never is a USA Today bestselling author of dark and contemporary romance. Her females are fierce and her alphas are magnetizing, just like the romance she provokes between them. She casts a spell, weaving one wonderous word at a time. A native of new Jersey, she is now a Maryland transplant juggling life the way one would juggle knives —carefully reckless. She has a dependence on sushi, a fetish for boots, and is stalked by a clingy pit bull named Apache. Writing is her passion, but readers are her love.

facebook.com/M.NeverAuthor

twitter.com/MNeverAuthor

instagram.com/m.neverauthor

ALSO BY M. NEVER

Books by M. Never

Owned (Decadence After Dark Book 1)

Claimed (Decadence After Dark Book 2)

Ruined (A Decadence After Dark Epilogue)

The Decadence After Dark Box Set (Books 1–3)

Lie With Me (Decadence After Dark Book 4)

Elicit (Decadence After Dark Book 5)

Moto: A MFM Ménage Romance

Trinity: A MMF Ménage Romance

Ghostface Killer

The Southern Nights Series

Stripped From You (Stripped Duet #1)

Strip Me Bare (Stripped Duet #2)

www.mneverauthor.com

#ProvocativeRomance

33863016R00128

Made in the USA
Middletown, DE
19 January 2019